"What do you want from me, Vivian?"

Rafael looked up, his black eyes gleaming in the soft light.

"I don't know," she whispered, unsure what else to say.

"That's a cop-out."

"It's the truth."

"I don't think so." Rafael withdrew his hands from hers, only to wrap them around her elbows. Then he pulled Vivian toward him until her face was mere inches from his own. "I think you knew exactly what you wanted when you came back in here." He pulled her a little closer. "It's the same thing I've been wanting since I felt you pressed against me on that damn bike tonight."

Vivian's heart nearly exploded in her chest, it was beating so fast. But she didn't pull away. She couldn't. Because Rafael was right. Damn the rules of professional conduct, damn staying uninvolved, damn the fact that they were from two different worlds. Vivian knew what she wa... ...e consequences.

Dear Reader,

I'm so excited to be a part of Harlequin's sixtieth anniversary celebration, especially since they've been a part of my life for as long as I can remember. My mother—who has been reading Harlequin romances since she had to cross into Canada to get them—handed me my first book when I was in fifth grade. I devoured it in one afternoon, and was well and truly hooked. Over the next few weeks, I read all of the other Harlequin books on her shelf and was completely thrilled when the next month rolled around—and a whole new crop of books came available.

This is my third book for Harlequin and, as I write this letter, I can't help remembering the ten-year-old I was and the Diana Palmer novel that opened my eyes to a whole new world of happily ever after. How could that young girl possibly have imagined that twenty-two years later she'd be writing love stories for that very same publisher?

A Christmas Present is a story of love and redemption, preconceptions and unexpected surprises. I really enjoyed creating a novel that concentrated on the themes of the holiday season—family, forgiveness, hope and second chances. Rafael and Vivian have a long way to travel to get to their happy ending, but I think the trek is a heartwarming one, and I hope you feel the same.

Thank you so much for letting my vision of Christmas into your hearts. I love to hear from readers via my Web site, www.tracywolff.com or on my blog, www.sizzlingpens.blogspot.com. I hope you enjoy reading *A Christmas Present* as much as I enjoyed writing it. Drop me a note and let me know what you think.

Merry Christmas and Happy New Year!

Tracy Wolff

The Christmas Present
Tracy Wolff

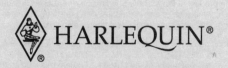

HARLEQUIN®

TORONTO • NEW YORK • LONDON
AMSTERDAM • PARIS • SYDNEY • HAMBURG
STOCKHOLM • ATHENS • TOKYO • MILAN • MADRID
PRAGUE • WARSAW • BUDAPEST • AUCKLAND

Recycling programs
for this product may
not exist in your area.

ISBN-13: 978-0-373-71607-4

THE CHRISTMAS PRESENT

Copyright © 2009 by Tracy L. Deebs-Elkenaney.

www.eHarlequin.com

Printed in U.S.A.

ABOUT THE AUTHOR

Tracy Wolff collects books, English degrees and lipsticks and has been known to forget where—and sometimes who—she is when immersed in a great novel. At six she wrote her first short story—something with a rainbow and a prince—and at seven she forayed into the wonderful world of girls' lit with her first Judy Blume novel. By ten she'd read everything in the young adult and classics sections of her local bookstore, so in desperation her mom started her on romance novels. And from the first page of the first book, Tracy knew she'd found her lifelong love. Now an English professor at her local community college, she writes romances when she's not chasing after her three young sons.

Books by Tracy Wolff

HARLEQUIN SUPERROMANCE

1529—A CHRISTMAS WEDDING
1568—FROM FRIEND TO FATHER

Don't miss any of our special offers. Write to us at the following address for information on our newest releases.

Harlequin Reader Service
U.S.: 3010 Walden Ave., P.O. Box 1325, Buffalo, NY 14269
Canadian: P.O. Box 609, Fort Erie, Ont. L2A 5X3

To Emily Sylvan Kim,
for your friendship, guidance and always
available shoulder to cry on.

CHAPTER ONE

VIVIAN WENTWORTH WALKED down Ellis Street as fast as her four-inch stilettos could carry her. Head up, eyes alert, she clutched her leather briefcase in one hand, while the other—tucked into the front pocket of her coat—was wrapped securely around a small canister of pepper spray. She ignored the catcalls and crude comments that came from seemingly all directions, cursing her boss, and the judge who had kept her late at court, with every rapid step she took.

"Hey, lady. Are you lost?"

Ignoring the tough-looking teenager who stank of alcohol and sweat was extremely difficult, particularly when he had planted himself directly in her path. But ignore him she did, shifting her body a little to the left to keep from brushing up against the dark-haired youth as she passed.

This whole thing was a bad idea. A really horrendously bad idea. She'd known it right away, but Richard had been immovable. The firm needed to take on more pro bono cases, needed to raise its profile for community service in a city that took activism to a whole new level. Why she'd been selected as the guinea pig for the new program, she didn't know. But Richard had insisted—they *had* to take this specific case, *had* to help this specific shelter, and she, specifically, was the one who *had* to do it.

She sighed in disgust. She had nothing against pro bono cases, having taken on quite a few in the six years since she had passed the bar. Nor did she hold a grudge against homeless boys accused of murder.

But she wasn't a defense attorney. She was a *divorce* attorney with a very full plate, and most of her past pro bono cases had been for local women's shelters, helping their residents escape abusive marriages with something more than a bunch of physical and emotional scars.

What did she know about mounting a defense in criminal court, save what they had taught her in law school over six years before? Even then she'd known she wanted to be a divorce attorney, so she hadn't exactly dedicated herself to the criminal law courses. How on earth could she help this boy when she didn't have a clue what she was doing herself?

It wasn't fair, not to her and not to Diego Sanchez. If he truly was innocent, as Richard claimed, then he deserved more than an attorney who hadn't been in a criminal courtroom since her first internship. And if he was guilty, then she took offense at wasting her time defending anyone who could callously and brutally rape and murder a pregnant, sixteen-year-old girl.

Vivian glanced at her watch, knowing what it would say before she saw the little hand sliding past the seven. Court had run over by nearly an hour, which meant that she was hugely late for her appointment with Diego. She hated being late to anything, let alone a client meeting. It was particularly hard to swallow tonight, as her lateness was what had put her in the unenviable position of being hassled by this teenager in the street.

A part of her couldn't help wondering if Diego got his jollies the same way this boy seemed to, though she did her best to ignore the thought.

Maintaining her air of confidence was getting more difficult by the second, but Vivian was determined not to let anyone around her know just how uncomfortable she was walking in this particular area—filled with prostitutes, drug dealers, gang members—as day slowly drifted into twilight. But as the short kid who had spoken to her was joined by a couple of friends and the trio began to trail her down the street, she grew increasingly alarmed.

Taking a deep, bracing breath, she straightened her shoulders a little more and sped up—a task that was more than a little difficult in her skyscraper heels. At another time, this tableau might have been funny, especially since she stood about three inches taller than the tallest boy. But here, now, it wasn't the least bit amusing. It was frightening and disconcerting, and she wanted nothing more than for them to give up and leave her alone.

Not that she thought there was a chance in hell of that happening.

Her hand clenched more tightly around the pepper spray. It was a weak weapon when faced with three drunk or high teenage boys bent on God only knew what, but it was better than nothing.

Besides, it was her own fault. She'd known better

than to come down here in her court clothes. The Tenderloin area of San Francisco was famous—or should she say notorious—for the danger lurking on the streets any time of day. Like anywhere, though, night was when the predators came out and the streets were at their most dangerous—so dangerous, in fact, that even the police rarely showed up here after nine o'clock.

She'd planned on going home to change before the meeting, had hoped to wear something a little less conspicuous. Of course, she'd also hoped to take a taxi, which would have delivered her straight to the door of Helping Hands. Instead she'd taken the BART train to a station three blocks from the shelter and then trusted in human goodness that she would make it to the door unharmed.

Trust wasn't her strong suit at the best of times, and tonight was a perfect example of why.

Glancing at the building to her right, she tried to decipher the address through the grime without slowing her pace…1097, thank God! Only a little farther and she'd be at 1055 Ellis Street. Hopefully the community center would be a lot safer than the dilapidated neighborhood it existed in.

Though she'd grown up in San Francisco, she'd never been to this area before—her parents would have quiet heart attacks if they knew she was here now.

"Hey, lady. Whatcha need? I can show you where to get whatever you want." The dark-haired kid reached out and grabbed her elbow, spinning her to face him before she could make a move to stop him.

His words bounced around her brain as Vivian struggled to make sense of them. "Nothing." Her voice came out as a croak. "I don't need anything."

He gestured down the street. "My cousin's got whatever you're looking for. He'll even cut you a good deal, since you're so hot and all." His friends laughed as he leered at her, his rancid breath invading her air space.

She struggled not to gag as the overwhelming smell of booze hit her head-on and his meaning finally sank in. Drugs. He thought she wanted *drugs*.

Pushing away the sympathy that welled instinctively, Vivian twisted her arm, struggling to break his grasp. "Really, I'm fine. I don't need anything. I'm just trying to get—"

His leer grew more pronounced at her denial. "Well, if you're not looking for smack, what *are* you looking for? There's only a couple reasons women like you come down here. If it's not to get high…" He let the implication dangle as he crowded her, pushing her against the front of the abandoned building as his lower body—his very hard, very aroused lower body—bumped into her own.

His friends moved in behind him, flanking him on either side and cutting off any viable means for escape.

Anger exploded inside of her, a wild animal raking her with sharp claws, making her heart pound faster and her breathing spiral out of control. Any sympathy she'd had for them evaporated as she vowed not to go down without a fight.

She tried to break away, to bring her arms up between the two of them and push the kid back, but he was stronger than he looked. And she was hampered by the tight skirt of her suit and her total lack of experience with physical brawling. She'd never been in a fight in her life and she had no idea what to do to get out of this one.

She couldn't even use the pepper spray, as he was holding on to both her arms, the weight of his body pressing against hers until she was all but immobile, and completely vulnerable.

"Look," she said, her voice trembling so badly she could barely understand herself. Determined not to show him how afraid she was, she cleared her throat and tried for a steadier tone. "I'm sorry. I just want to get to the community center. I'm supposed to—"

He reached up, grabbed her breast and began to squeeze. "The community center, huh? You'll get there. Eventually." His laugh was low and mean, and his two companions joined in.

Vivian twisted against him, preparing to scream as she looked around frantically for help. But violence was a way of life down here, and the few people near her either didn't notice her plight or didn't care enough to risk their own lives by interceding.

She continued to struggle against her attacker, trying to get her hand free so she could actually use the stupid pepper spray. Her movements only excited him more— she could see it in his eyes, hear it in his suddenly ragged breathing. Feel it in the hardness pressed between her thighs.

Nausea overwhelmed her, burning away the anger and leaving terror in its place. So much for those stupid self-defense classes she'd taken. Nothing they'd taught her was working, and she was suddenly very afraid that she wasn't going to be able to find a way out of this.

His hand moved from her breast to her skirt, and he started to push the raw silk up and out of his way. Fear cut through the fury and tears welled in her eyes before she could stop them, trembling on her lashes before spilling down her cheeks.

"Please." She looked him straight in the eye, struggled to reach the lost kid inside the street tough. Struggled for her own safety and sanity. "Please don't do this. I beg you, please. Stop."

For a second she thought she'd reached him, thought she saw his eyes soften as his hand stilled. But then his friends laughed and one commented, "You were right, Nacho. The rich ones don't mind begging at all."

She glanced at the third boy. He looked scared, nervous, as though he wanted to be anywhere but where he was, though he never opened his mouth, never said a word.

Nacho's eyes hardened, the brief look of compassion dying out as if it had never been there. "That's right. Didn't I tell you I know how to treat a woman? By the time I'm done she'll be beggin'…on her knees."

He gave a sharp tug and Vivian felt her panty hose rip. She did scream then, one long, thin burst of sound as she struggled violently. When she finally got her left hand free, she brought it to Nacho's face and scratched long furrows down his cheek even as she continued to buck against him. Trying desperately to get to the pepper spray, to dislodge his grip on her skirt. To get away.

Nacho swore as her nails raked his face, and brought his hand back to slap her. His friends crowded in and Vivian closed her eyes, bracing for the blow she knew was coming.

But it never landed. Suddenly she was free, and Nacho and his friends were simply gone. "What do you think you're doing?" It was a new voice, deep and husky and so authoritative it got her attention instantly.

She opened her eyes in time to see Nacho stumble back against the wall. Glancing around wildly, half expecting his friends to attack in his place, she was shocked to see them sprawled on the dirty sidewalk and sidling backward slowly, their eyes fixed on the newcomer's furious face.

Not that she blamed them—she'd never seen anyone or anything like him in her life. Even as she straightened her clothes, her precarious situation hanging heavily over her head, she was painfully aware of him and the power he wore like a second skin.

He was huge, towering over her despite her own impressive height. He was built like an ancient warrior, and normally his wide shoulders, broad chest and narrow hips would have made her nervous as hell. At this particular moment, however, she couldn't be more grateful for his strength and obvious command.

Looking up into eyes so deep and black she swore they could belong to the devil himself, Vivian took an uncertain breath, then pressed a trembling hand to her heart as she fought to breathe around the relief pumping through her. His gaze swept her from head to toe, one long look that must have assured him she was unharmed, because he turned back to her would-be attacker.

"Since when do you get your kicks beating up women?" he snarled as he hauled the kid up, his face inches from Nacho's suddenly young and frightened one. "I thought you knew better than that. If you want to fight, why don't you pick on someone you don't outweigh by fifty pounds?"

Her savior's fingers tightened into fists and the kid started to back away. "Hey, Rafa, chill. We were just havin' some fun. Playing with the *gringa*."

"Fun?" His voice dripped disgust. "That's the kind of fun that'll get you arrested, Nacho. Or killed." His voice was low, the threat unmistakable.

"Hey, no way, man. I wasn't really going to hurt her." Nacho shoved against the newcomer hard and ran, his friends trailing quickly behind him.

Her rescuer turned his head, pinned Vivian with a look that was both dark and intense. "Do you have a cell phone?" he asked.

Caught in the act of fumbling her crumpled skirt back into place, Vivian repeated dumbly, "A cell phone?"

"To call the cops?"

Her teeth were chattering so badly she almost couldn't speak. "The cops?"

"Never mind." Reaching down, he grabbed the briefcase she had dropped during the scuffle. "We'll call from my place. I'm just up the block."

As the haze of terror wore off, Vivian's brain began working again. "I don't think—"

"Relax," he said, with a grin that was more a baring of teeth than an actual smile. "I own the community center. You'll be safe there."

"Community…" Things began to sink in as she walked toward him. "Oh, you're with—"

"Helping Hands." He nodded, placing his palm

gently on the small of her back as he guided her down the sidewalk. Any other day she would have shrugged him off, but her knees were still knocking together and the support felt good.

"Are you hurt?" he asked as he propelled her toward the center.

"I'm fine." Her voice was a little higher than she would have liked, but the nervous adrenaline coursing through her made her regular tone impossible.

"Are you sure? I can call an ambulance." He glanced at her. "It might be a good idea to do that anyway."

"No, really. I'm good, just a little shaky."

They continued walking in silence for a few moments and Vivian struggled to compose her thoughts. She didn't usually need to be rescued, and it pricked her pride that he thought she was so fragile that she required an ambulance to keep from freaking out.

But pride or not, she owed him a thank-you. Clearing her throat, she said, "I don't know what would have happened if you hadn't—"

His low sound of exasperation surprised her. "Yes, you do."

"I'm sorry?" She stopped dead to avoid slamming into him as he suddenly turned to face her.

"Look, you're young and attractive and walking down this street wearing clothes worth more than I make in a month. We both know exactly what would have happened had I not shown up when I did." He stepped in front of her, pulled open a door and waved for her to precede him.

"I didn't plan it this way," she protested. "It just happened."

He snorted, clearly unimpressed. "Famous last words."

Annoyance was rapidly starting to replace her gratitude, but because he'd saved her from getting raped—maybe even killed—she bit her tongue as she stepped inside the building.

The front room was huge, the walls painted a sunny yellow and interspersed with various murals that ranged from the amateurish to the surprisingly sophisticated. Whatever she'd been expecting, this mixture of color, comfort and smiling faces wasn't it.

Overstuffed sofas and chairs were scattered around the room and a huge television took up part of one wall. A few teenagers sat around it, playing a video game. Others were gathered around the pool and foosball tables that sat in the center of the room, while still others were draped comfortably on a couple of the sofas, talking and passing an iPod back and forth between them.

A huge Christmas tree stood in the corner of the room, decorated with sparkling lights and hundreds of homemade ornaments, some of which looked almost professionally done. There were other hints of Christmas around the big room—wreaths on the doors, poinsettias near the front desk, and what looked like mistletoe hanging in one of the tall archways.

She shook her head, more than a little intrigued. As far as teen centers went, this one was a lot more inviting than most. It also looked as though it was a lot better funded, and its patrons were remarkably well-behaved.

"Hey, Rafa, I kicked your butt, man." One of the kids near the TV called to her rescuer. "I'm already two thousand points above your record."

Rafa laughed. "Enjoy it while you can, Marco. You know it won't last."

"Yeah, we'll see. Soon you will *bow* before the master."

"Don't hold your breath. I forgot to renew my CPR certification this year."

The kids around Marco snickered, but he merely shrugged good-naturedly. "You're all talk, man."

Rafa paused to watch as the boy maneuvered a famous skateboarder through one incredible stunt after another. "Nice job, Marco," he commented as a huge grin replaced the frown he'd been wearing since the moment she set eyes on him. "You might have me, after all." He turned away, then called over his shoulder as he headed down the hall. "For a day or so."

Vivian stared after him in amazement, unable to make her feet move for long seconds after he'd walked away. The man's smile was a lethal weapon—it lit up his face from the inside out and showed her a side of her rescuer she hadn't dreamed existed. She started to follow him, her stomach once again uncomfortably shaky.

Maybe that perpetual scowl of his wasn't such a bad thing, after all.

RAFAEL GLANCED BEHIND HIM at the woman trailing him down the hallway to his office. She *had* to be the lawyer—who else would be walking down the most dangerous street in San Francisco dressed like *that* and looking for his community center? She was late and would have been even if Nacho and his band of moronic maniacs hadn't hassled her. But then, Rafael shouldn't be surprised. Experience had taught him that women like her were never on time, even if a young boy's life hung in the balance.

Maybe especially then.

As he opened the door to his office, his upper lip curled with a disgust he didn't even try to hide. Diego needed a real lawyer, someone who understood him and where he came from. What he didn't need was this slick Barbie doll version, who spent more attention on her clothes and makeup than she ever would the poor, pro bono client her law firm was forcing her to help.

When he'd called in the favor owed to him by one of the center's board members, he'd expected Richard Stanley to send an experienced trial attorney. Someone who was acquainted with his kids' way of life. Someone who was willing to dig in for a fight, and didn't look like she was born with a glass of champagne in one hand and a designer handbag in the other.

Instead, Richard had sent this…cupcake, and now Rafael had absolutely no idea what to do with her.

"The bathroom's through there." He gestured to a door behind him and to the right. "If you want to clean up."

"Oh, right, thanks," she murmured, obviously still a little dazed from her close call. Unless the blank eyes were part of her normal demeanor, in which case Diego was in a lot more trouble than he'd originally thought. And that was saying something.

"I'll just be a minute."

Rafael nodded as he picked up the phone and dialed the local precinct. He figured he'd have plenty of time to call the cops and check on the kids— women like her didn't know the meaning of "just a minute." She'd be in there checking out her appearance for a while.

Not that there was anything wrong with how she looked, despite her close call with Nacho. Rationally, Rafa knew that part of his anger at her stemmed from her total lack of regard for herself.

Everything about her was a come-on. From her long, long legs and her do-me heels to her slender curves and chili pepper red hair, she screamed for attention. Add to that skin as pale and creamy as his mama's flan and her made-for-sex mouth, and the woman was a walking wet dream for the wolves roaming the Tenderloin's dark streets.

Still, despite the fairy princess looks, something about her bugged him. Something that wouldn't fit into the mold he imagined she fit—

The door to the bathroom swung open and she stood there, as beautifully put together as she would have been for a charity ball. It irked him, had him slamming the phone down on the third ring.

He would call Jose later—have the detective run by and scare the hell out of Nacho and his band of merry morons. The boys weren't going anywhere. Rafael shook his head. It wasn't as if they had anywhere else *to* go. Right now, he had enough to deal with between the lawyer and Diego.

The lawyer cleared her throat as she walked carefully into the room, her back ramrod straight and her limbs flowing sensuously with every step she took. No wonder the boys on the street had been all over her—she looked like a goddess and walked like a ballerina. Was there some school rich girls went to that showed them how to walk like that or was she just a natural?

"I want to thank you for rescuing me. I'm grateful—"

"I don't need your gratitude."

"I know. But that doesn't mean I don't feel it." She reached into her briefcase. "I'd like to do something to say thank-you. Maybe make a donation to—"

He shoved the bag back down. "I don't need your money, either."

"I didn't mean it like that."

"Sure you did." He made sure his smile cut like glass. "But there are some things in life that can't be bought. I'm one of them."

Silence stretched between them, and his nerves started to twitch before she finally broke it.

"All right then." She held her hand out. "I'm Vivian Wentworth."

"I know. Rafael Cardoza." Instinct had him meeting her palm with his own, though he regretted it the second he touched all that soft, smooth skin.

"Well, then, I assume you know why I'm here." She glanced around. "Where's Diego?"

"Upstairs. Working." Rafa leaned down a little until his face was only inches from hers. "I want to make one thing perfectly clear. I don't know why Richard sent you. I don't know what he expected someone like you to be able to do for Diego."

"Someone like me?"

"You know what I mean. You look like you spend more time in a salon than you do in a courtroom." Even as he said them, he couldn't believe the words had left his mouth. He was acting like a total bastard, but he couldn't afford to be nice. Diego was too important for him to put the kid's fate in the hands of a lawyer who didn't know what she was doing.

"I can assure you I have seen my fair share of courtrooms," she snapped. "And then some."

"Yeah, well, excuse me if I'm not rolling in confidence here. You don't exactly look like the type to care about what happens to a poor Hispanic kid accused of murder—even if he is innocent. "

She stiffened, her eyes darkening, and for a moment he would have done anything to take back the words. There was no call to speak to a woman like that. His mother would have had his ass.

But Vivian Wentworth, Esquire, handled his shit like a champ. She simply nodded and said, "Then it's a good thing he's got me, isn't it?"

It was the first indication Rafael had that he might have underestimated her. But not the last.

CHAPTER TWO

OUTRAGE EXPLODED THROUGH her and, for the second time in less than an hour, Vivian understood what it was to want to do violence. She would like nothing more than to beat this smug, self-righteous idiot to a bloody pulp. Yes, he'd rescued her, but one act of kindness didn't make up for the rest of his boorish behavior.

"I'm a very good lawyer, Mr. Cardoza, and I give one hundred percent to all of my clients, whether they're pro bono or not."

"I didn't mention anything about you taking the case pro bono, Ms. Wentworth. Funny that that's where your mind went automatically."

Gritting her teeth, Vivian kept the smile on her face through sheer force of will. "Facts are facts." She glanced at her watch pointedly. "And we're already over an hour late getting started. I'd like to see my client now."

"About that…"

She felt her shoulders tense a little bit more, and braced for the verbal blow she had a good idea was coming. He didn't disappoint her. "Don't push him. Diego's really broken up about this whole thing, and I won't put up with you running around, messing with his head."

"Messing with his head?" She couldn't keep the incredulity out of her voice. "Mr. Cardoza, your client is accused of murder and stands to spend most, if not all, of his life behind bars. Of course he's worried—"

"I didn't say worried." The look on Rafael's face was as sharp and deadly as an ice pick. "I said he's broken up. His girlfriend and baby are dead and he's devastated. I won't put up with you making that worse."

"I'm here to help Diego, not make things worse."

"That remains to be seen, doesn't it?" He tossed the words over his shoulder as he headed for the door.

She closed her eyes and took a few deep, calming breaths. Murder was against the law, she reminded herself with every exhale. If it wasn't, she wouldn't be here trying to deal with this utterly impossible, completely deplorable man. She counted to ten and waited for the urge to strangle him to pass. Or at least mellow.

A huge part of her wanted to quit before ever getting started. It wasn't as if she didn't have lots on her plate with the numerous divorce cases she was currently handling, as well as her work at the women's shelter. Besides, it was bad enough having to battle the entire legal system for a kid accused of a vicious crime, without having to battle his prickly protector, too.

She sighed heavily. Quitting wasn't really an option. Rafael obviously had some kind of pull with Richard or she wouldn't be here. Her boss could spout off about helping the community all he wanted, but getting personally involved wasn't his typical modus operandi. Like her mother—and most of the other rich people she knew—he just wrote a big check to charity twice a year in the law firm's name and considered his duty done.

But this time he'd gone out of his way to take the case and to hand-select her for it. For whatever reason, Richard had felt that she was the best choice for this job, and she wasn't going to disappoint him. She'd worked too long and too hard these past few years to get him to notice her as something other than Steven and Lillian's daughter. Vivian would *not* blow this chance, no matter how ill-equipped she felt dealing with it.

She started down the hall after her reluctant rescuer. Hell would freeze over before Rafael Cardoza got the best of her, and the sooner he figured that out, the better off they both would be.

RAFAEL SMILED GRIMLY to himself as he escorted Vivian upstairs to one of the classrooms currently being renovated. Round one might have been a draw, but she wasn't nearly as cool as she wanted him to believe. For one very brief second in his office, he'd seen fear flicker in those crazy, violet eyes. And while it had made him feel like a heel, it had also given him a small sense of satisfaction. She should be afraid, especially if it made her pay attention to her own safety. Nob Hill was a long way from here, in attitude and life lessons, if not location.

Silence stretched between them, the only sound the click-click of her ridiculous shoes as she climbed the old concrete stairs. It gave him a perverse kind of pleasure to keep her guessing about their destination, not willing to let her in on it until she asked.

As they reached the third-floor landing, he risked a

side glance at her and wondered again how she was supposed to help Diego. The kid needed someone tough, someone who wouldn't back down, and Vivian looked like a strong breeze would knock her over. How the hell was she supposed to stand up to all the crap circulating about this case?

How the hell was she supposed to stand up to the establishment when she *was* the establishment? Everything from her wardrobe to the way she walked screamed old money—and a lot of it.

Just then, the door to one of the classrooms flew open and Diego strode out, his simple black T-shirt spattered with yellow paint. "Rafa," he said, his face lighting up when he saw them. "I'm just about done in here. You want to take a look?"

"Absolutely." He patted the kid's shoulder. "You did a great job with the other two."

"Thanks." He gestured for Rafael and Vivian to precede him into the room.

Rafa looked around the freshly painted space with satisfaction. "It looks good. Real good."

He wasn't lying, either. Diego had talent for making over rooms that seemed hopeless. He'd spent the last few days in here repairing the holes in the walls, painting and hanging up bulletin boards and whiteboards. He'd even sanded the floor, and the old wood gleamed under the fluorescent lights.

"Esme thought it'd look good in yellow," Diego whispered, his face a mask of misery and fear. "She was right."

The kid's sorrow made Rafael want to punch something, preferably the scumbag who had killed Diego's girlfriend and unborn child. "You'll make a hell of a handyman." He turned to Vivian. "Diego wants to start his own company when he graduates in a few months."

"That's wonderful," she commented, with a sincerity that surprised him.

"Is that—" Diego stopped midsentence and put on the I-don't-give-a-damn attitude that had gotten him into so much trouble to begin with.

Rafael grimaced as he watched the transformation, but said simply, "Diego, this is Vivian Wentworth. Ms. Wentworth *this* is Diego."

Vivian reached a hand out and grasped the one Diego offered almost reflexively. "It's nice to meet you, Diego. Rafael's right—the room looks wonderful." Her smile was warm, her eyes watchful, and Rafael couldn't help the kick in his gut that came with the first real upward turn of those luscious, lopsided lips. He ignored it, focused on Diego instead.

"Thanks. Rafa's been paying me to help him out." The kid's voice was stilted and frightened. Rafael wanted to wrap his arms around him—this scared, special kid who was still more boy than man—and keep him safe from this nightmare he was experiencing. "I was saving to pay—" He broke off, his throat suddenly working convulsively.

"For the baby?" Vivian's voice was soft, persuasive. "And for Esme?"

Diego stared at the floor, unwilling—or unable—to look her in the eye. "Yeah. But that's gone now." His voice was flat, unemotional, despite his recent loss.

But she could see the pain in him. The harsh lines that

bracketed his mouth and looked so out of place on his young face. The dark circles that shadowed his eyes. His careful body movements, as if one wrong move would shatter him. She remembered the feeling from when her older sister had died, and Vivian's heart went out to him, this boy who'd been forced into manhood too soon.

As she looked at him, every instinct she had said he hadn't done what he was accused of. Not this sweet, harmless kid with yellow paint on his fingers and heartbreak in his eyes. He couldn't have brutally raped and murdered his pregnant girlfriend. Not when it was obvious he'd have preferred to die with them.

"I'd like to talk to you for a few minutes," she said. "Find out exactly what happened that night."

He nodded his head, cool and collected except for the tremor in his hands. "I told the cops—"

"I know," she interrupted. "But I'm not the cops. I'm your lawyer and I'm on your side." Against her better judgment, she reached over and laid a hand on his elbow. The kid just looked so lost.

Of course he's lost, she told herself. It had only been two months since everything he cared about in the world had been wrenched away from him. Less than that since he'd been arrested.

"That's what the public defender said when he urged me to take the deal they offered. He said I wouldn't get a better offer."

"And you probably won't." She'd already been over his file—twice—and had familiarized herself with the assistant D.A. who had his case. The man didn't like to plea-bargain, had only offered to do so on this case because some of the evidence was shaky and Diego was under eighteen. She remembered enough from law school to know that that combination was often good for the defense.

"Not from Gallagher." And not with the amount of interest the press was taking in this case. If she wasn't careful, they'd have Diego tried and convicted before any of them ever set foot in a courtroom.

"But I didn't do anything! I couldn't hurt Esme. I would *never* hurt her. Or my baby." Diego looked as if he was going to cry. "I loved her. We were gonna get married before the baby was born, as soon as I'd saved up enough money to get an apartment for us."

"It's all right, Diego. Vivian can't make you take the plea bargain if you don't want to." Rafael shot her a look, one that promised retribution, when she hadn't done anything wrong. "And he *doesn't* want to," he added in a hard voice.

"I never suggested that he should take the plea bargain. I'm not in the habit of sending innocent boys to jail, no matter what you might think of me, Mr. Cardoza." She was proud of the icy tone she'd managed, when what she really wanted to do was tell him to go to hell. For someone who had asked for help, he sure didn't act as if he expected her law firm to be able to deliver.

But then he didn't know her. Didn't know that there was no way she could let Diego be convicted if there was some way she could prevent it. Something about his utter vulnerability, the pain he couldn't hide, struck a chord in her she hadn't realized existed.

Rafael's eyebrows rose incredulously. "So you believe him?"

She raised hers in mocking response, completely fed up with the attitude he kept throwing at her. "Don't you?"

"I would have left him in the hands of that incompetent public defender if I didn't." The man's expression said that he wasn't sure she was any better, which angered her, even though she agreed with him on a base level. But he didn't know she wasn't a defense attorney, so he had no right to his ridiculous opinion. And she refused to apologize for the fact that her life, so far, had been pretty damn good.

Refusing to rise to the bait any more than she already had, Vivian smiled at Diego as Rafael escorted them to a room at the end of the hall that had a table with a bunch of chairs scattered around it. "The first thing I want to know," she commented, pulling out a notepad to record the conversation, "is how come your P.D. didn't apply to have the case heard in juvenile court? You're only sixteen, right?"

"Mr. Williams said the judge wouldn't move it. The crime was too big a deal and I'm too close to eighteen."

"'Close' only counts in horseshoes and hand grenades," she muttered, shaking her head in disgust. She might not know her way around the criminal justice system the way Diego's P.D. had, but she recognized laziness when she saw it. "We're going to give it a shot."

"Why?" Diego asked. "Wouldn't it be better to try my case in front of a jury?"

"Who told you that?" she demanded.

"Mr. Williams."

She shot Rafael a disgusted look. "I take it you're the one responsible for getting rid of this guy?" she asked.

He snorted. "Every single thing that came out of his mouth struck me as idiotic."

"That's the smartest thing you've said all evening." She turned back to Diego, but not before she saw the flash of annoyance in Rafael's eyes. Good, let him be on the receiving end of the digs for a while. She'd had enough of his nasty attitude and nastier comments. It was past time for her to get a little of her own back.

Resting her hand gently on top of Diego's, she turned her back on his mentor and said, "The evidence in your case is far from rock solid."

"Because I didn't *do* it."

"I know," she answered soothingly. "But that's why we want you in front of a judge in the juvenile system. Judges look only at the evidence, while juries, despite their best intentions, are often swayed by photographs and emotions." She made sure she was looking into his eyes before continuing. "The photos in this case are particularly brutal, so—"

"I saw them." This time he couldn't hold back the tears.

"When?" she demanded, suddenly furious. "Williams didn't—"

"No, not him. The police made me look at them, when they questioned me."

"What did your lawyer say?"

"I didn't have one then."

She stared at him. "You were questioned without an attorney? Were your parents there?"

He shrugged. "My family, we're not real tight like that. I've been staying here for the past few months."

Her gaze shot to Rafael. "Were you there?"

He shook his head grimly. "I was out of town when all this went down. Diego sat in jail for four days until I got back and found out about it."

"This whole thing has been a joke from start to finish." Vivian rubbed her hands over her tired eyes. "I need you to walk me through this whole thing."

"Can't you just read the file?" Rafael objected. "He's already told the story a bunch of times."

"I have read the file, Mr. Cardoza, but I need to hear it from him. Besides, he needs to get used to telling it, as he'll be saying it again and again—to me, to the judge and to whomever else I deem necessary."

She turned to Diego. "I know it's hard to talk about what happened to Esme and your baby, but I need to know everything. Don't leave anything out, no matter how insignificant you think it might be. At least not now, not with me."

She held her hand up when Rafael started to protest, and in the steely voice she reserved for deadbeat dads and abusive husbands, said, "You went through a lot of trouble to get my law firm to take this case, so why don't you cut the guard-dog routine and give me a chance to do my job? Otherwise you should have stayed with Williams."

"He trusts me and I'm not going to let you waltz in here and turn him inside out for your own enjoyment."

Her mouth dropped open before she even had a shot at finding her poker face, and she finally felt her temper snap. "My own enjoyment? Look, you jerk, I can think of a lot of things I'd enjoy more than sitting here listening to a child talk about murder, but I don't have that option. And neither does he. Not if we want to win this thing." Out of the corner of her eye she saw Diego's eyes widen and his hands clench, and she forced herself to take a few deep breaths as she worked to regain her composure. No matter how she felt about Rafael, Diego trusted him. "I assume that's what we all want to do, isn't it?"

Rafael refused to answer, but he didn't object when she asked Diego, "When was the last time you saw Esme alive?"

He cast an uncertain look at the man, but started to speak when his mentor nodded at him. "About four o'clock, on the day she died."

"January 12."

"Yeah. I took her to her doctor, for her checkup. She was six months and pretty big, so he did another ultrasound. Just to check out the baby, you know?"

Vivian nodded and he continued, his fingers tapping a nervous rhythm on the scarred conference table. "But everything was cool. He was growing like he was supposed to, swimming around in that amni—amni—"

"Amniotic fluid," she supplied.

"Exactly. Esme's weight was good, her blood pressure, everything. So he sent us home, told us to make an appointment in two weeks."

"This was at the clinic on Washington, right?" she asked, glancing up.

"Right." He wiped his hands on his jeans, his foot

tapping in the same rhythm his fingers had been following a minute before. "I took her home and then headed
over here. I had work."

"Did you drive her home?"

"I don't have a car. We took the bus and then I walked
with her from the bus stop."

"Did you see anyone you knew?"

"Where?"

She shrugged. "I don't know. On the bus. On the
walk home. At her building."

"I guess so. I never really thought about it."

"So think about it now. Who did you see?"

His eyes narrowed as he concentrated. "I saw Nacho
and Luis—they live in the building next to Esme's."

"Nacho?" She glanced at Rafael for confirmation.

He nodded. "Same kid."

Diego looked at her questioningly, but let it go when
she didn't pursue the matter. "Anyone else?"

He thought for a second. "Esme's oldest brother Ric.
He was leaving when we were going in."

"Did you talk to him?"

"Just said hello, you know? Nothing big. He and
Esme don't—didn't—get along."

Her antennae went up. "Really? Why not?"

"I don't know. Esme pretty much thought he was a
jerk, so we didn't talk about him much."

Vivian lifted her head, studied him carefully. "She
never said anything about him? Never complained to
you about him, never talked about buying him a birthday
present? Nothing?"

"Well, sure, that kind of thing. But nothing major."

"So tell me what she did say."

"Everything?" he asked incredulously.

"Sure. Whatever you remember."

"I don't remember much. I mean, we were together for two years, so she said a lot about him, I guess."

"You just said she never talked about him."

"We never really had a conversation about him. Just stuff she said in passing."

"Like what?"

"I don't know. Like he'd dropped out of school to deal drugs for a while. Like she didn't like the guys he hung around with, even before the dealing started."

"You're telling me Esme's brother is a drug dealer?" she asked, just to clarify things.

"They both are. Nothing major, though. Just some weed and X, that sort of thing."

"Ecstasy?"

He looked at her as if she was stupid. "Well, yeah."

"And the cops know about this?"

"I guess so."

"You didn't tell them?" She couldn't keep the shock out of her voice.

"I figured they knew. What's the big deal, anyway?"

"The big deal is there's nothing in their report about it. I can't believe they didn't at least look at them."

"For Esme's *murder?*" Diego asked. "Ric and Danny wouldn't do that."

She pinned him with her best glare. "I thought you said you didn't know Ric very well?"

"I don't. But I didn't get any crazy murder vibes off him, either."

"I didn't realize every killer radiated 'crazy murder vibes,'" she commented. "It must make the police's job so much easier."

"Vivian." Rafael's voice held a warning.

She glanced at him, saw his jaw tighten, and decided not to push Diego about Esme's brother. At least not right now. "Okay. So did you talk to anybody else that you can remember?"

"Just Lissa, Esme's best friend. She came over as I was leaving to head to work."

"She's the one who found Esme's body later that night."

He nodded stiffly, then started drumming on the table again, his rhythm faster now that he was more agitated.

"How did you find out that Esme was dead?"

"Lissa called me on my cell phone, after she'd called 911."

"And you rushed right over."

"Of course I did. I loved Esme and our baby. I didn't want to believe her."

Vivian doubled back. "And you came straight here after taking Esme home?"

"Yeah."

"What time did you get here?"

"About four-fifteen. Her apartment's only a couple of blocks away."

"You were here the whole time?"

"Yes!" His voice got louder, more insistent, but she didn't try to calm him down. Not now.

"Who saw you?"

"A bunch of people."

"So why don't you have an alibi?"

"I was up here working most of the time."

"By yourself?"

He shrugged. "Yeah. Rafa gave me the job, but the center can't really afford to pay a bunch of us, so I come in every day and work for a few hours. Do what I can."

"And you didn't leave?"

"No."

"Didn't take a break? Go downstairs and get some dinner? Go to the restroom? Nothing?"

"I went to the bathroom, but up here." He pointed down the hall. "There's a bathroom near the stairs."

"What time did Lissa call you?"

"Around ten-thirty that night. She told me that I had to come right away." He looked down at the table, shame in every line of his body. "I hassled her. Things were coming along really well here and I didn't want to be interrupted.

"I was here, patching the walls, painting, thinking about an essay I had to write for school, while Esme was dying! How could I have been doing that, while some animal was hurting her?"

THERE IT WAS, Rafael thought, the question that had been haunting the kid for the last nine weeks. Well, that and who had actually committed the murder Diego was charged with. Rafa knew Diego hadn't harmed Esme— he wasn't capable of it, could barely bring himself to squash a spider, let alone brutally rape and murder the girl he loved.

"How could you have known, Diego?" When he spoke his voice came out gruff with misuse. It had been hard to sit here, keeping his mouth shut, while somebody else took over with Diego, but he knew enough about the system to know it was necessary. And for the first time since he'd gotten back to town and found out Diego had been arrested, he felt as if the kid had a chance.

For all of her fashion magazine looks and cool, cultured voice, Vivian Wentworth seemed to know her stuff. Her questions had been fair, incisive and structured to give her the whole picture of the situation. He could admire that, especially since it seemed to indicate that Diego would get the defense he deserved.

And the look in her eye—the one that had messed with his head back in his office?—he'd finally identified it. Behind the mascara and shadow, her eyes held the gleam of a warrior, one who didn't like losing.

It was the same look he'd seen in the mirror any number of times since he'd decided to change this old warehouse into a teen center. The same look that had gotten him through all the fundraising and city council meetings it took to keep this place going. The same look that convinced his board to let him do things at the center his way.

It was nice to see that Vivian had some of that same fight in her. She was going to need it before this thing was over.

Rafael had a hard time trusting anyone—couldn't stand being out of control enough to let someone else do what he couldn't—but as he watched her with Diego, he thought he just *might* be willing to bet on Vivian doing what was necessary to protect the boy.

CHAPTER THREE

THE QUESTIONS WENT ON forever, until Diego's eyes were drooping with exhaustion and even Rafael felt as if he'd been put through the emotional wringer. The only one who looked no worse for wear was Vivian, whose voice was as calm and compassionate now as it had been when she'd started questioning Diego two hours before.

As Diego went over details of his relationship with Esme for the second time, Rafael let his mind wander for a minute. Then was brought back to the present with a jolt as Vivian started gathering up the copious notes she'd taken.

"I think that's all for tonight," she said as she slipped the papers into her briefcase. "But I'd like to meet again in a couple of days, after I've had a chance to research some things."

"Sure." Diego stood, wiping his palms on his jeans before extending a hand to her. "Thanks, Ms. Wentworth."

"You're welcome, Diego. But we're just getting started—there's a long road ahead of us."

"Yeah, but you're the first person, besides Rafa, to really listen to what I had to say about everything. I really appreciate that."

Vivian smiled, and Rafael was struck again by her sincerity. Though he hated to admit it, he might have been wrong about her. Maybe this was more than just a toss-off pro bono case to her. Maybe—

He cut his thoughts off with a grimace. It was early days yet and there was a lot to do before Diego even had a chance of getting out of trouble. Yet Rafael couldn't help looking at Vivian differently as he escorted her downstairs.

"Where's your car parked?" he asked, his voice rusty from hours of disuse as he'd sat back and let Vivian do her thing.

"I took BART."

"Are you telling me you walked all the way from the BART station in this neighborhood? I thought you'd just parked on the next block or something. Are you crazy?"

As soon as the words slipped out he wanted to take them back. Not because he didn't mean them, but because her back turned as stiff and unyielding as a fireplace poker. But damn it, was she insane? She was lucky Nacho and his gang were the only trouble she'd run into.

"No, Mr. Cardoza, I am *not* crazy. I was however, running late and didn't have time to go home for my car. As I take BART to work every day, I was stuck with that option to get here. Believe me, I wouldn't have been wandering the streets at dusk if I could have avoided it."

Her explanation soothed him, despite it being delivered in the prissiest tone he'd ever heard. Or maybe because of it. Something about her cultured tones and incredible composure got to him—not to mention that fantastically crooked mouth with its too-full upper lip.

Made him wonder what she'd sound like if he mussed her up a little bit…or a lot.

"Do you mind if I wait here for a cab?" she asked in a voice that suggested it wasn't the first time she'd asked him the question.

He shook his head to clear it, then watched her root around in her briefcase for her cell phone. "You'll be waiting all night. You won't catch a cabbie within three miles of this place once the sun goes down."

"Are you sure?"

"Pretty sure, yeah." He paused, then did what he'd known he was going to do all along. "I'll drive you home."

Her eyes darted to his. "You don't have to—"

"Yes, I do, and we both know it. So can the obligatory protests and let's go." He headed toward the back of the shelter, and the alley where he kept his bike, without waiting to see if she followed. It wasn't as if she had any other option.

A quick stop by his office yielded an extra helmet, and then he was pushing the back door open. The cold December air rushed by him, making him shiver despite his leather jacket.

He glanced behind him. If he was cold, Vivian must be freezing in her thin suit. "Here," he said, as he shrugged out of his jacket. "Put this on."

She eyed the jacket uncertainly for a moment, then reached for it and slipped it around her shoulders. "Thanks. I appreciate it…. Where's your car?"

He laughed, then nodded to the motorcycle parked a few feet away. "We're not taking a car."

"No car? But…" He watched her closely, taking

perverse pleasure in the shock—and discomfort—that flitted across her face as she noticed the motorcycle for the first time. "We're not riding *that,* are we?"

"Sure we are. Now take the helmet." To her credit, she did as he told her. He chose to ignore the fact that it was probably due to her surprise rather than any desire to actually get along with him.

"Are you sure—" Her voice broke and she had to start again. "Are you sure this is the only way to get me home? I mean—"

He laughed, then swung his leg over his prize Harley. "Relax. It's a million times easier than riding a bicycle." When she still didn't move, he glanced at her impatiently. "Get on."

She just stared at him—and the bike—warily. But then the wind picked up, blowing hard between the buildings and making her shiver all over again.

"Just swing your leg over the seat like I did," he said.

"Um, sure. But…"

"But what?" He fought to keep the impatience out of his voice, but he was cold, tired and more than a little hungry, since he'd skipped both lunch and dinner to deal with center business. He knew his annoyance had leaked through when she stiffened.

"What do I do with my briefcase?" She held up the brown leather bag she was carrying.

"I'll take care of it." He grabbed it and started to shove it into the saddlebag of his bike, shocked at just how soft and supple the leather was. The thing had probably cost thousands of dollars—just one more thing to underscore the differences between them.

Not that he should care about those differences. Not that he *did* care about them, he told himself. He finished buckling the saddlebag and said, "Now climb on."

Muttering beneath her breath—too low for him to hear what she was saying, which was probably a good thing—Vivian did as she was told. It wasn't fast and it wasn't pretty, but eventually she managed to get herself situated behind him. He was proud of himself for not laughing.

"Now hang on," he said, as he started the bike.

"To what?" she yelled over the sudden roar of the engine.

He did laugh then as he glanced behind him in disbelief. "To me!"

It was the last thing he said before he slipped the bike onto Ellis and sent it roaring into the night.

VIVIAN TIGHTENED HER ARMS around Rafael's waist and tried not to scream as they sped through the nearly empty streets. It wasn't easy, when every shift and shimmy of the bike had panic racing through her.

When Rafael laughed as he careened around a corner, barely slowing the motorcycle down, she knew with absolute certainty that she had indeed gone crazy. Why else would she have her arms wrapped around a man who despised her as they barreled through the night toward certain death?

Except it wasn't nearly as bad as she'd expected it to be. The smooth purr of the engine was kind of exciting, especially if she didn't think about being completely unprotected in case of a crash. If she just focused on the wind whipping past her and the soft sway of their bodies as they rode through the night, it was almost relaxing. Even before she added in the strong, resilient warmth of Rafael's back, which she was currently pressed against intimately.

It was amazing that a man with such a nasty disposition could have such a comforting way about him. She'd noticed it first when he'd saved her from Nacho and his friends, and then when he was calming down Diego. Now here it was again as they were pressed breast to back, inner thigh to hip.

He was like a furnace, the heat his body emanated absolutely amazing, especially since he didn't have a jacket on. Yet somehow he managed to keep her warm throughout the wild ride, so warm that when they finally arrived at her apartment complex and she climbed off the bike, she somehow felt bereft without the contact.

It was stupid, ridiculous, yet something about being wrapped around Rafael had made her feel safer than she'd felt in a long time. Shocked and more than a little frightened of the feeling, she found her voice came out more abruptly than she would have liked.

"Thanks for the ride. And the rescue earlier. I appreciate it." She took off the helmet and held it out to him.

He didn't reach for it right away, instead choosing to pull his own helmet off and study her. His eyes gleamed black in the rosy glow of the streetlight, and for one long moment she was trapped. Caught. Unable to move or think or do anything but feel as his eyes swept leisurely over her from head to toe.

Her heart started to pound and her knees trembled—actually trembled—under the weight of his gaze. It was that small shake that jump-started her brain and had her backing away from him as panic skated down her spine.

She didn't need this, didn't want this—with any man. Certainly not with a man who despised her very existence.

"Don't worry about it." His voice was low and gruff. "But bring your car when you come on Thursday. You can park around back where I keep my bike. It should be safe there."

"Sure." She looked over his shoulder, then down at the ground, anywhere but into those black-magic eyes that were somehow holding her in thrall. "Um, same time? Seven o'clock? That way, even if court runs late, I won't be."

"Sure. And, Vivian?" He paused and silence stretched between them, so long and tense that finally she had to look up. As their gazes collided, she realized it was what he'd been waiting for. "Thanks for helping Diego."

Shock almost had her jaw dropping before she caught it. "I thought—"

His smile, when it came, was rueful. "I was wrong. I thought you were there to go through the motions, that you really didn't care—"

"Of course I care!" The words burst from her. "Do you think I want to see that poor child go to jail for the rest of his life? For a crime he didn't commit?"

"I know, I know." Rafael held out a hand as if to soothe her, but stopped just short of touching her. Yet she could still feel him, though she didn't know how. Or why. "That's why I wanted to apologize. I really appreciate what you're trying to do for him. We both do."

She shook her head. "Don't thank me. It's my job."

She took off his jacket, surprised at how much she wanted to keep it, then pressed it into his hands.

He took it reluctantly, shoved it into his saddlebag after he'd returned her briefcase to her. Then he pinned her with a look so fierce her heart jumped in her chest.

"I don't think so." He pulled his helmet back over his head. "I think it's you."

He started the bike and roared away before she could come up with a suitable reply.

Head swimming, feet aching, Vivian stumbled into the lobby of her apartment building. Michael, the doorman, greeted her with a smile she returned. He rushed to call the elevator for her, as he always did when she came in late.

She rode up to the penthouse condominium her parents had bought her when she'd graduated from Harvard Law, summa cum laude. It had been a bribe to get her to come back to San Francisco, and one she hadn't been able to resist, despite the numerous job offers she'd received from a variety of New York and Washington firms.

But San Francisco, with its turbulent ocean and temperamental weather, was home.

The second her apartment door closed behind her, she kicked off her shoes with a sigh of relief. She had an addiction to expensive, high-heeled shoes, and normally her feet handled her little problem just fine. But after eighteen hours in the four-inch heels, even her steel arches were weeping.

Shrugging out of her suit jacket, she dropped it on the kitchen table on her way to the refrigerator. A little spurt of guilt raised its ugly head, but she shoved it down. The house didn't need to be spotless all the time, no matter what her mother said; Vivian could hang the jacket up tomorrow.

Right now it was—she glanced at the clock in the breakfast nook—almost eleven-thirty and the turkey sandwich she'd gulped down for lunch between court sessions had long since worn off. She wanted a quick snack and about eight hours stretched out on her very comfortable bed. But tomorrow was Tuesday, and one of the two mornings a week she spent volunteering at a battered women's shelter. She could cancel and try to get some extra sleep, but everything inside her rebelled at the thought.

They needed her. When she'd finally become an adult, she'd sworn she'd never turn her back on someone who needed her. Like Diego. That boy—

The phone rang, interrupting her train of thought, as she was haphazardly slapping a couple pieces of cheese between two slices of bread. She started to reach for it, but just didn't have the energy to deal with anything else tonight, no matter how irresponsible that made her.

When the answering machine finally kicked on and her mother's voice flooded the room, she was glad exhaustion had won out over conscience.

"Vivian, this is your mother. Are you really not there? It's eleven o'clock. If you're out, I hope it's on a date and not with one of those women for the shelter. You know, the Winchester boy has been asking about you and I told him you were available. I think he might be calling, so be nice when he does. The Black-and-White

Ball is coming up fast and I mentioned that you didn't have an escort yet. Remember, I helped organize it again this year so I expect you to be there. *No* excuses.

"Also, I was calling to see if you had time to go Christmas shopping next Tuesday. I thought we'd make a day of it—brunch, shopping, maybe an afternoon at the spa. Your nails were looking so ragged the last time I saw you, and your hair could certainly use a little pick-me-up. And don't give me any nonsense about work— I don't think you've taken a day off in two years. Call me and let me know what time you would like to meet on Tuesday. I'll be home tomorrow until eleven."

The answering machine clicked off abruptly.

Vivian carried her sandwich into the family room, but instead of sinking onto the nearest available space, she went to stand near the long picture window that over-looked the nearly infinite Pacific.

Nothing like her mother to put things in perspective. *Forget the women's shelter—you should be on a date. Forget helping others—we should go shopping.*

Shopping was her mom's answer to everything, and it always had been. Bad day at school—let's go to the mall. Break up with a boy—a new dress is just what you need. Your sister died—Nordstrom's is having a sale. Let's go.

Vivian fought the old bitterness that crept up, hating the way her mother could so easily cut her off at the knees. She reminded herself that her mother felt things in her own way, and that criticizing her daughter was how the woman showed her love. Dwelling on how Vivian wished things were different wasn't going to do anything, Lillian Wentworth would always be exactly what she was.

Dispassionate, formal, unwilling to show emotion, which was exactly what she'd raised her daughters to be. Thank God the lessons hadn't rubbed off, at least not on Vivian.

Still, her skin felt too small for her body, as it often did after she'd heard from her mother. Her stomach—which had just started to relax—was in even tighter knots than it had been on the back of Rafael's motorcycle. But then, Lillian was good at getting Vivian all worked up, good at making her feel vulnerable and inferior and disappointing.

Sometimes she wondered if her mother had been taught her passive-aggressiveness at Vassar along with all the core subjects. So many of her friends had the same ability….

As she crossed to the sofa, Vivian took a bite of her sandwich, but it tasted like sawdust now. Shoving it away, she draped her legs with the violet afghan one of her pro bono clients had made her. Then reminded herself of how much luckier she was than Diego or Marco, or any of the other kids she'd seen at Helping Hands earlier that night. She had a home, a career she loved, a family who had provided for her materially, if not emotionally.

The fact that she had spent her life wanting more just proved how selfish she was. And how lonely.

CHAPTER FOUR

"HEY, ARE YOU GETTING OLD, *mi hermano?* You're play-ing like you've got arthritis."

Rafael flipped his oldest brother, Miguel, the bird before backing up just enough to send the ball soaring into the basket for three points.

"Hey, look at the tall guy taking advantage." This came from Jose, his teammate and best friend. After everything that had happened to Rafael, it probably should have felt weird to have a cop as a best friend, but they'd been buddies since they were in elementary school together.

Besides, Jose was cool like that—he'd hung by Rafa during his time in prison, despite the crap he'd caught from other members of the force.

"That's right." With a grin, he watched Jose intercept the ball, then cruised down the court for the pass. Jose didn't disappoint, and as soon as Rafa had the ball in his hands, he blew around the opposite team—com-posed of his two older brothers—and slam-dunked the hell out of it.

Jose whooped. "That was game point, my man!" He looked at Rafa's middle brother, Gabriel. "You owe us twenty bucks, *Papi.*"

"I thought gambling was illegal," Gabe grumbled good-naturedly as he reached into the back pocket of his shorts and pulled out a ten. "Go hit Miguel up for the other half."

"You know I will!" Jose danced away, talking shit and blowing smoke like he did every time they won. Or lost.

"So, Máma wants to see you." Gabriel glanced at Rafa, then took a large gulp from his water bottle.

"What else is new? Is there anything specific or is it just time for another 'you're my youngest child and I won't be happy until you settle down' lecture?"

"I'm sure there'll be a little of that in there, too." He smiled when Rafael cursed. "But I think she wants your help planning a surprise party for Miguel." He nodded at their brother, who currently had Jose in a headlock.

"Seriously? She really wants something to whine about other than how empty her arms feel without my baby in them?"

"I think so, man."

"Why me? Aren't the girls the ones who she usually gets to help with stuff like this?"

"Yeah, but Carolina's a little busy with baby number three right now, and Michaela's still recovering from pneumonia." He stepped back and looked his youngest brother over. "Besides, freak boy, you won't even need a ladder. That's what you get for growing so big."

Rafael grabbed a towel to wipe his face, decided to accept defeat gracefully. Maybe if he brought his mama flowers and kept her busy, she wouldn't remember to nag him about being the only one of her children who was terminally single.

Yeah, right. His mother wouldn't let a little thing like death stop her from hassling him—why should a bouquet of flowers do the trick? Still, Rafa thought as he drained a water bottle in one long gulp, it was worth a try.

"All right. I'll call her."

"You're a good man." Gabriel clapped him on the shoulder. "So, winners buy lunch, right? Because I'm starving."

This time it was Jose who flipped him the bird, having extracted his head from under Miguel's arm.

"Well, come on then, I've got to be back at work in half an hour and I'm hungry, too." Miguel picked up his bag from the side of the court and headed into the center.

A few minutes later they were all seated at Manuel's, Rafa's favorite hole-in-the-wall taco shop, shoveling carne asada burritos into their mouths. Rafa had already blown through his first when he noticed Nacho standing at the corner with an unfamiliar white boy.

"Hey, Jose. Did you get a chance to talk to Nacho about what he pulled the other night?"

Jose followed his gaze. "Absolutely. My partner and I went by and read him the riot act. Hopefully, it'll be enough."

Rafa cut his eyes to his best friend. "You don't think so?"

"No, man. That kid's a walking time bomb."

"That's what I think, too."

"Who's he with?" Miguel nodded at the prepped-out white kid. In his chinos and fancy sweater, he stuck out like Rudolph the Red-nosed Reindeer. "Is he one of your kids, Rafa?"

"No, but he seems familiar." He continued to watch him, wondering what the kid was doing in this neighborhood—and with Nacho. "That doesn't look good, though." He turned to Jose.

"I know. But I can't see Nacho buying any of his customers lunch."

"He's dealing?" This from Gabriel.

"That's what I hear."

Rafael cursed. "You know that's not a good thing. The kid's already an amoral ass. I can't wait to see what a few months as a dealer turns him into."

"I think it's too late to worry about that." Jose took another big bite.

"I know. But still…" Rafa ran a hand over his eyes. *You can't save them all,* he reminded himself. *Especially the ones who aren't interested in salvation.* It grated that a teenager was going bad in front of his eyes. He still remembered Nacho as a little kid. He'd been skinny and mean even then, but there'd been something endearing about him, anyway. Now he was just plain mean.

Regardless, Rafa couldn't help wondering if the rest was still there, too, just buried beneath the crap. On his way out of the restaurant, he stopped by the table. "Hey, Nacho. Who's your friend?"

"Screw you, Rafael."

"Thanks, but you're not my type." He held out his hand to the other kid, who shook it, but then looked as if he wanted to swim in a vat of hand sanitizer.

Rafa didn't get what these two were doing together, but he'd bet the twenty in his wallet that it had something to do with the drugs Jose had been talking about. "We're having a barbecue at the center this weekend. You guys should drop by."

"Yeah, 'cause that's going to happen," Nacho sneered.

"Too busy picking on defenseless women to make time for a hamburger, huh?"

"Too busy avoiding *pendejos* like you."

"Well, that's your prerogative." He looked at the preppy kid. "Nice to meet you…?'

"Thomas."

"Thomas," he repeated. "Maybe I'll see you around."

"Maybe."

As Rafael hustled to catch up with the rest of the guys, he couldn't shake the feeling that he'd seen the new kid before. Anymore than he could ignore how uncomfortable that knowledge made him.

"THANKS SO MUCH FOR seeing me today." Vivian extended her hand to each homicide detective in turn. "It's nice to meet you both."

"Same here." Detective Anthony Barnes nodded to her, a lock of his too-long, sand-colored hair falling over his baby face as he did so. He looked younger than Diego, and the idea that this guy had arrested her client for murder threw her for a major loop.

"You want some coffee?" demanded Daniel Turner, the other detective, even as he raised a hand to signal the waitress.

"That'd be great," she said, though she'd already had an entire pot of the stuff that morning. But she didn't want to seem prickly, especially since these two had been nice enough to meet with her when other detectives would have turned up their noses.

She smiled at Turner, and was glad to see that he, at least, looked like her idea of a homicide detective. A little overweight, a little rumpled, with lines in his face that showed every one of his forty-odd years, he seemed like he'd been doing this job for a long time.

"Thanks again for meeting me," she said, in an effort to keep everything cordial. "I know how busy you are."

"That's okay." Turner shrugged. "We wanted to get a look at the woman who was defending that piece of scum, anyway."

Maybe he'd been on the job too long, Vivian thought, as sheer strength of will kept a pleasant expression on her face. "So, you're really convinced Diego did it?"

"We're not in the habit of arresting people for murder if we think they're innocent." The detective's voice was deliberately bland.

"Of course. I wasn't trying to imply that you did. It's just that after reviewing the case, so much of the evidence seems circumstantial to me."

"Enough circumstance adds up—if you know what I'm saying."

"I do. But still, why Diego? I know you always look at the boyfriend or husband first, but sometimes he isn't the killer."

"Most of the time he is." Turner reached for one of the little packets of half-and-half and ripped it open. "In this case, Sanchez is definitely it. He's practically got a scarlet A branded into his chest."

"Why? Witnesses say they saw him drop the victim

off at her house at least a couple hours before she was murdered."

"Yeah, but that doesn't mean he didn't circle back," Barnes interjected. She glanced at him and was surprised at how uncomfortable he looked, as if he'd rather be anywhere but in this crappy little coffee shop.

Deciding to push him, she replied, "It doesn't mean he did, either. It seems to me he really loved that girl."

"Yeah, well, appearances are deceiving. If you learn nothing else in this foray of yours into criminal court, learn that," Turner said, before Barnes could speak.

"Oh, I think that's a lesson I've already learned." Vivian smiled sweetly at him as she let her eyes run over him from head to toe.

He flushed. "Good. Because no one else had motive, means and opportunity." He tore open two packets of sugar and dumped them into his coffee, then took a huge swig without bothering to stir it.

"Means?" she asked as she went over the file in her head for what felt like the millionth time. "I didn't see anything in the case file about you finding the murder weapon."

"I don't need a weapon. That kid was popped for carrying a knife before he was twelve years old. He definitely knows his way around a switchblade."

"Yes, but the case was dismissed as self-defense. Besides—"

"Self-defense, my ass. Is that what he called murdering his unborn kid?" Turner snorted, then shook his head as he repeated, "Self-defense."

"Besides," she said again, "Diego hasn't been in any

trouble since then—no fights, no problems at school, no drugs. His school counselor seems to think he's had a pretty rough time of it."

"Yeah, well, the vic sure as hell didn't have an easy time of it either. Pregnant at sixteen, living with two of the scummiest dealers in—" He stopped abruptly, but it was too late and he seemed to know it.

Vivian was careful to keep a neutral expression as she seized on the opportunity Turner had inadvertently provided.

"So, you *do* know Esme's brothers deal drugs?" She made sure to direct the question to both detectives, then watched as Turner's face turned beet-red. But his reaction wasn't nearly as interesting as Barnes's was. The young detective started drumming on the table with the same nervous energy Diego had displayed when she was questioning him a few nights before.

Trying to capitalize on his obvious discomfort, she leaned forward and asked softly, "Why didn't you at least look at the brothers—or their rivals—when Esme turned up dead, Anthony?"

"We did." Once again it was Turner who answered. "There was nothing there."

"Nothing there? They're gang members and drug dealers, and both have been in and out of the system for years. How can there be nothing there?"

"Because they didn't kill her!"

"Maybe, but what about other gangs? Other dealers? I hear there's always a turf war going on in this neighborhood."

"What do you know about this neighborhood?"

Turner didn't bother to hide his contempt. "You're over here doing your little pro bono case, and as soon as it's done you'll run as far and as fast as you can back to where you belong."

"Where I'm from is not the issue here."

"Well, it should be. You do-gooders are all alike. You come over here thinking you can save some kid who doesn't deserve to be saved. Maybe you save him, maybe you don't, but either way you make life ten times harder for the victim's family while you're doing it. And then you just walk away."

"What about arresting an innocent man?" she asked quietly. "How does that affect the victim's family?"

Turner's face went from red to purple, and for a second Vivian feared he might be having a stroke, but when he spoke, his voice was steady and poisonous. "I wouldn't know. Your client did it and he's going down for it. He'll be lucky if he doesn't get a needle in the arm by the time the D.A.'s done with him. Killing a pregnant woman counts as special circumstances."

"Yes, well, the judge didn't think that scenario was very likely. Otherwise Diego never would have had a chance to make bail." She gave as good as she got, refusing to back down.

"Look, lady, we've got motive, means and opportunity. That's a slam dunk."

"Really? Because when I was looking through the file, it seemed to me that you had nothing. What's the motive again?"

"He didn't want the baby. According to Esme's friends and brothers, Diego was getting cold feet."

"These are the same brothers that we've already established deal drugs?" she asked. "The ones with the shady rivals?"

"That doesn't make them liars."

"No, but it doesn't make them paragons of reliability, either. What else have you got?"

"He could come and go any time from Esme's place—that's opportunity."

"Yeah, but nobody saw him there and he has an alibi."

"Somebody did see him—the woman who lives across the street—and his alibi's shaky."

"So's your evidence, but you don't see me whining about that, do you? Your witness is a ninety-three-year old Chinese woman with cataracts. If I paraded Santa Claus in front of her, she'd finger him as the killer."

"But she didn't finger Santa Claus, did she? She fingered your client."

"Because he was the only Mexican in the lineup. I can't wait to see what a judge has to say about that."

Turner shook his head in disgust. "Jesus, you're just as bad as all the other defense attorneys, you know that? I thought a divorce attorney might have more sense."

She started to snap back another smart-ass comment, but then his words sunk in. "How do you know what kind of lawyer I am? I never mentioned it to you."

"What, are you keeping it a secret?" Turner shot his partner a furious look and then pushed back from the table. "This conversation is over. And don't call me again. If you want to talk to me, you can do it in court." He stormed off.

Barnes smiled awkwardly as he stood. "Sorry about that, Ms. Wentworth. He gets a little excited sometimes."

"It's fine." She studied him for a second, more than a little intrigued by his discomfort. "Tell me something, Anthony. If Turner hadn't been pushing for it, would you have arrested Diego Sanchez for murder?"

"Absolutely." His voice was firm, resolute, but his eyes never made it past the bridge of her nose. "I have to go now."

"I know. Thanks again for meeting me."

"No problem." He reached into his pocket for his wallet, but she stopped him.

"Don't worry about it—coffee's on me. It's the least I can do after pulling you down here for nothing."

He didn't say anything, just nodded and walked quickly away.

Vivian watched as Barnes pushed the door open, then continued observing him through the front window as Turner caught his arm outside the diner and said something with an ugly look on his face.

Turner's defensiveness was definitely interesting, almost as interesting as Barnes's inability to look her in the eye. She wasn't sure what any of it was about. It could be nothing, just their standard operating procedure, but her instincts were telling her there was a lot more to their behavior—and this case—than met the eye.

Digging in her briefcase for her cell phone, she dialed the office.

"Stanley and Baker, Vivian Wentworth's office. How may I help you?" Her assistant's chirpy voice came through loud and clear.

"Hey, Marcy. I need you to get one of the investigators on something for me."

"Sure, Viv. Let me grab a pen…. Okay, shoot."

"I want to know everything there is to know about SFPD homicide detectives Anthony Barnes and Daniel Turner. They operate out of the Tenderloin Station, on Eddy Street."

"Got it." Her voice dropped. "Is this about that case Richard gave you? The pro bono one?"

"Yes."

"You know, reporters have been calling all morning to talk to you. They want a statement."

"Of course they do." Vivian was disgusted at her own stupidity. It wasn't exactly a surprise the press were interested when the city's top law firm filed papers with the courts to defend such a violent crime. The miracle was that it had taken them two days to discover what she'd done on Tuesday morning.

"What did you tell them?"

"That you were presently hard at work on the case and would contact them as soon as you had had a chance to look over all the evidence."

"You're a lifesaver. I'll get a statement written up tonight, and you can e-mail it to everyone tomorrow."

"Great, I'll tell them that and maybe it'll get everyone off my back a little."

Vivian laughed. "Don't count on it."

"I won't." There was a pause. "Oh, Viv, how do you want me to pay the investigators? Does it come from your office accounts or…"

"I didn't even think of that." She paused, sorted through her options. "Look, tell them to bill us for now, and I'll talk to Richard this afternoon about how much leeway he'll give me in terms of expenses for the case. If worse comes to worst, I'll pay for it myself. Either way, I want that report on my desk by the beginning of next week."

"Got it."

"Oh, and call Rafael Cardoza at Helping Hands and ask him if I can push tonight's meeting until seven-thirty. I have a few things I need to do this afternoon before heading over there."

"Sure."

"And check in with Jenny and see where she is in drafting the complaint over the police questioning Diego without representation. E-mail me with her answer."

"Is that *all?*"

Vivian laughed. "For now. I'm due in court in forty minutes."

"Good luck—not that you'll need it. The Markison case is in the bag."

"From your mouth to God's ears."

After she hung up with Marcy, Vivian took a sip of her forgotten coffee, then wished she hadn't. No wonder Turner had been adding cream and sugar left and right—the stuff tasted like paint thinner.

Pushing the coffee aside, she leaned back in her chair and tried to make sense of all the pieces of Diego's puzzle she'd managed to gather in the last few days. But she couldn't do it. Too many things about this case stank to high heaven.

Barnes's nervousness.

Turner's determination that Diego was guilty, despite the lack of a murder weapon or definitive proof.

Esme's brothers' extracurricular activities.

The D.A.'s offer of a deal—as pathetic as it was—on such a high-profile case.

Richard's assignment of a divorce attorney to a case that needed a very skilled defense attorney, especially when the press were breathing down everyone's neck.

She rubbed a hand over the tight muscles of her own neck. This case was a disaster waiting to happen. And she didn't have a clue how she was going to avert it.

WHERE THE HELL WAS DIEGO? Rafael checked his watch for the third time in as many minutes. Diego was late, really late, and that just wasn't like him. The kid was conscientious to a fault, always showing up on time, never taking off work so much as five minutes early. The fact that he wasn't where he was supposed to be now meant something bad had happened.

Rafael could feel it.

For the second time that night, he scoured the center for the kid. But Diego wasn't in the game room, or the kitchen, or outside on the basketball courts. He wasn't taking a shower or hanging out in Rafa's apartment as he sometimes liked to do.

He wasn't *anywhere*.

Stressed-out and more than a little concerned, Rafael bounded up the back stairs for the second time, checked the classroom Diego had been working, then searched all of the other rooms up there as well, hoping like hell Diego had decided to start work on one of them instead of checking in first, even though he'd never done that in the past.

But by the time he got to the last classroom, Rafa was forced to acknowledge again that Diego wasn't there. Worry gnawed at his stomach, a painful ache that was growing with each passing second.

Why wasn't Diego where he was supposed to be?

And what the hell was Rafael supposed to tell Vivian when she showed up? He glanced at his watch yet again. It was seven twenty-five and he could only imagine what she would think if her client was a no-show.

Part of *him* couldn't help thinking the worst, and he knew the kid better than anyone.

Had Diego freaked out and fled, worried that he wouldn't beat the case? Sure, he was mature and smart and pretty levelheaded for a seventeen-year-old, but he was still just a kid. One who had lost everything that mattered to him except for his freedom.

Had he taken off in a desperate effort to preserve the illusion of that freedom? But spending his life running, always looking over his shoulder, was just a different kind of prison. One Rafael prayed Diego would never have to experience.

Damn it, how was he going to find the kid if he *had* run?

And if he hadn't run, then where the hell was he? Rafael paced the long hallway outside the second floor classrooms as his mind whirled with possibilities.

Had Diego been mugged? Jumped? Shot? The sad fact was a lot of things could happen to a person in this neighborhood, from walking into a corner drug deal to interrupting a robbery.

Diego had grown up on these streets, but that didn't mean he wasn't vulnerable, especially after being arrested for Esme's death. Right now, he could be lying somewhere in a pool of his own blood....

The thought galvanized Rafael into action, had him taking the steps three at a time and then whipping through the game room as if the hounds of hell were on his heels. And maybe they were. If Diego had been hurt—

"Still no sign of Diego?" he called on his way through.

A chorus of no's greeted him, then one of the new girls—Lupita, he thought her name was—called, "I haven't seen him since yesterday."

That wasn't what Rafael had wanted to hear.

He yanked open the center's front door, barreled through it without looking, and ran straight into Vivian. The impact had her teetering in the ridiculous heels she liked to wear, and he grabbed her elbows to steady her.

"Are you all right?" he demanded gruffly, bending down so they were eye to eye. "Did I hurt you?"

"I'm fine. Just a little surprised." She pushed away from him, ran a hand over her tightly restrained hair. "So, where are you going in such a hurry?"

Her voice was smooth, like the silver tequila his mama kept for special occasions, and ripped right through him despite the precariousness of the situation. She sounded as smart and put together as she looked, and while that would normally have made him happy, today it only made him worry more.

How the hell was he going to convince this intelligent, savvy woman that Diego hadn't run, when he couldn't even convince himself?

With a sinking heart, he turned and led Vivian back

to his office, all the while wondering exactly what he could say to convince her not to dump Diego.

Whatever it was, it had better be good.

VIVIAN'S KNEES KNOCKED together as Rafael's black eyes met hers. He looked as bristly and obnoxious as ever, as if those few minutes after the bike ride the other night had never happened.

She started to get her back up, to give as good as she got from him. But when she looked closer, she saw worry in his tense jaw and lowered brows. Her heart sped up in response.

"Rafael? Is everything okay?" She took a step toward him, glanced around. "Where's Diego?"

Was it her imagination or did he stiffen even more? A sick feeling started in the pit of her stomach, though she tried to tell herself she was being too sensitive. When Rafael opened his mouth to speak, only to close it before any words came out, she felt the sickness turn into something more. Something worse.

"Where's Diego?" she repeated, her instincts warning her that that was the root of Rafael's concern.

He stared at her for long seconds, then finally shook his head. "I haven't got a clue. I was on my way to look for him when you got here."

Her stomach clenched. "You were in an awful big hurry. Do you know something I don't?"

"I don't know anything. That's the whole point. Except that it's not like Diego to be late." Rafael strode over to his desk, picked up the phone and punched in a few numbers. There was a pause as he waited for whoever it was to answer, and then a spate of Spanish she couldn't understand.

"What did they say?" she asked as soon as he put the phone down. But he held up a hand to stop her, then repeated the process a second time. And a third.

When she felt she was going to burst if she didn't get some answers, Vivian reached across the desk and grabbed his arm. "What's going on? Who are you calling? What did they say?"

Rafael's mouth was grim, his eyes more so when he answered, "No one's seen him since yesterday. He wasn't in school today, and he isn't here. It's like he disappeared."

"How could he disappear?"

"I don't know."

"Do you think something happened to him?"

"I don't know." His voice got louder.

"Do you think—do you think he's hiding? This is a lot to deal with—"

"I don't know!" It was all but a roar. "I don't know anything, Vivian, that's the whole point. I haven't got a clue where Diego is or what he's doing or who he's doing it with. If I did, don't you think I'd find him and drag him back here? He knew about this meeting, knew how important it was that he didn't miss it."

His shoulders slumped, and for the first time since she'd met him, Rafael looked as lost and confused as she often felt.

A kernel of sympathy bloomed inside of her and she moved around the desk, laid a gentle hand on his shoulder. "Maybe he's just late?"

"Maybe." Rafael shrugged, his powerful muscles bunching beneath her palm.

"You don't think that's an option."

He started to say something, then just shook his head.

"Well, let's be logical about this then. Where had you planned on checking earlier, when you were rushing out of here?"

"His dad's house. The church down the street he likes to go to. His favorite restaurant two streets over."

"So let's do that."

"I just did—that's who I called. No one's seen him."

"Well, let's check somewhere else then. Surely there are other places he hangs out. Maybe someplace he used to go with Esme?"

"You want to help me look for Diego?" Rafael looked shocked.

"Why are you so surprised? Of course I do."

He leaned forward and those troubled midnight eyes probed her face, though she had no idea what he was looking for. "Why would you do that?" he finally asked, his voice little more than a whisper. "Wouldn't it be easier for you if he disappeared?"

She started to tell him to go to hell, but bit her tongue at the last second. Hadn't there been enough assumptions and anger between them already? "Rafael, I took Diego on as a client, which means I care about what's best for him. And if you think something's wrong, with him not being here, then I'm going to believe you. Obviously you know him a lot better than I do and—"

The classroom door burst open and one of the kids

she'd seen the other day rushed through it, a cordless phone in his hand.

Marco. She pulled the name out of her memory banks. The one who'd been playing the video game with the skateboarder and had teased Rafael about beating his score.

"Rafa, man, it's Saint Francis Hospital. They say they've got an injured kid there with your card in his pocket."

CHAPTER FIVE

RAFA LEAPED FOR THE PHONE, barking "Hello" before she could even process Marco's news. But she could see the fear in Rafael's eyes, a fear she knew was reflected in her own. If the hurt kid was Diego, what had happened to him? Whatever it was, it was bad—the urgency in Rafael's voice told her that much.

For a couple of minutes that felt like hours, he kept up a cryptic one-sided conversation, and when he hung up, anger had joined the worry and hurt in his face.

"Diego?" she asked as she reached for her briefcase.

"I don't know. Whoever the boy is, he's in the ICU, floating in and out of consciousness. Somebody found him a couple of hours ago, near Trujillo's, but whoever called it in didn't wait around to talk to the EMTs."

She had no idea what Trujillo's was, but figured now wasn't the time to ask, not when Rafael was already halfway out the door.

"Wait!" She took off after him, the feeling a new sensation, as she wasn't used to trailing anyone. "I'm coming with you."

"Go home," he retorted over his shoulder as he headed down the hallway. "I'll call you when I know something."

"That's bullshit. I want to know what happened as much as you do. And if the police have been called, he'll need an attorney there."

"He's the *victim*."

"Yeah, well, he's also accused of murder. In a lot of precincts that supersedes any rights he might have, and I think you know that."

The grim look Rafael gave her said that he did indeed know what she was talking about. Probably better than she did.

He kept walking while they talked, swinging out into the alley without another backward glance. "We'll take my bike—it's faster."

Taking a deep breath, Vivian shoved down any reticence she had about getting on the thing again, then grabbed up the helmet she'd worn the last time and slipped it over her head before climbing onto the motorcycle. "Let's go."

He didn't say anything else as he swung onto the bike in front of her, but as he got ready to start it, he half yelled, "Hang on."

Like he thought she was suicidal? Despite enjoying her last ride, she was still more than a tinge anxious. Of course she was going to hang on—as tightly as possible.

Inching forward, she wrapped her arms around his waist and tried not to whimper when he whipped into traffic as if the devil himself was after them.

As Rafael weaved through cars, it occurred to her just how easy he'd taken it during their last ride. No quick lane changes, no darting in front of cars, no daredevil speeds. The same thing couldn't be said of him today as he raced toward the nearest hospital.

She stifled a curse as he cut off an 18-wheeler, then zipped between two lanes of bumper-to-bumper cars. He ignored the shouts and raised fingers in a way she couldn't, and finally she ended up closing her eyes and resting her head against his back to block out the insanity.

She stayed that way until she felt him pull to a stop.

As Rafael climbed off the bike, holding out a hand to help her off, as well, Vivian barely resisted the urge to fall to her knees and kiss the ground. Next time they were taking her car, and to hell with whether or not the motorcycle was faster. She'd pick slow and alive over quick and dead any day.

By the time she'd recovered her equilibrium, Rafael was once again striding away. Left with no other option than to scramble behind him like a lost puppy dog, she did her best to catch up.

The guard in the hospital lobby directed them to the elevators that would take them to intensive care. Once there the nurses simply got out of Rafa's way as he swept down the hallway toward the unknown boy's room. If she'd had a heavily muscled six-foot-six man dressed in jeans and black leather barreling down on her, she'd probably get out of his way as well, and to hell with the rules.

It wasn't until they turned the corner into the room that Rafael lost his momentum. The single-minded drive that had gotten him this far seemed to desert him, and he paused at the threshold as he gazed hesitantly at the bed. "Damn," he murmured, and as she turned her head to look at the victim for the first time, she understood what had shaken Rafael up.

The figure in the bed was almost unrecognizable as the boy she'd met the night before. His face was swollen and black-and-blue, his head bandaged. Both arms were in casts, and the fingers sticking out from the ends were as swollen and purple as his face.

"Oh, my God!" She crossed the room, reaching for Diego with trembling hands. She stopped herself at the last second, afraid that her touch would only hurt him more.

There didn't seem to be a spot on his body that wasn't bruised or broken.

"You poor baby," she murmured past the lump in her throat. "You poor, poor baby."

She glanced behind her at Rafael, who hadn't left his post by the door. His jaw was clenched so tightly she feared he might break his teeth, and his hands were curled into fists. His eyes were colder than she had ever seen them.

"Rafael." She spoke softly, tried to get him focused on her instead of the fury that had his big body trembling.

"They were trying to kill him. Whoever did this was trying to *kill* him."

The attorney in her had her cautioning, "We don't know that yet."

"Don't we?" He stalked forward until he was standing next to the bed. "Look at him."

"I know. But—"

Vivian broke off as a tall, blond woman in a white doctor's coat entered the room. "Are you Rafael Cardoza?" she asked, her voice wary.

He tensed. "I am."

"My name is Sandra Graham. I'm this boy's doctor. Do you know him?"

"His name is Diego Sanchez and I'm his court-appointed guardian."

"Excellent." She smiled at both of them, though she still looked a little nervous. "There's some paperwork you'll need to fill out when we're done talking. I'll have the nurse bring it to you."

"Will he be okay?" Vivian asked.

"I think so. But he has a lot of painful injuries and he needs time to heal—that's why I've put him into a drug-induced coma."

"What's wrong with him?" Rafael's voice was rusty.

"He's got a severe concussion and there's some swelling of his brain. It's perfectly normal in cases like these, but we'll be watching him closely to make sure it goes down in the next few days. He also has three broken ribs, one of which punctured his right lung. His left wrist and elbow are broken. His kidneys and spleen are bruised."

"Jesus. Is that everything?"

"Not quite." This time the doctor's smile was more a snarl. "He's also got numerous bruises and contusions, some of which needed stitches. Whoever did this to the kid knew what they were doing. They wanted to cause as much pain as possible, and they succeeded. He's going to be miserable for a quite a while."

"But he *will* be okay?" Rafael reiterated.

"He should be. He's young and strong, but, as always in ICU, the next twenty-four hours are critical. Let's wait and see how he responds when we bring him out of the coma tomorrow evening."

"Thank you." Vivian tried to smile, but inside she was breaking apart. It was stupid that within four days this kid had worked his way into her heart, but somehow he had. Not to mention that Rafael looked as if he'd been run over by a train. Twice. And for whatever reason, that hit her just as hard.

"You're welcome. Now, do you have any more questions before I send in the nurse?"

"No—"

Vivian cut off Rafael. "Actually, yes. Have the police been called?"

"They have. They came by and took a report, then said to phone them after he's conscious."

"Do you have a card or something with their names on it?"

"It's at the nurses' station. I'll have someone write the information down for you."

The doctor answered a few more questions before taking her leave. As the door swung shut behind her, Rafael collapsed into the chair by Diego's bed. "I'm going to find out who did this to him. And they're going to regret it," he growled.

His words had alarm coursing through her. Crouching down next to him, she laid a hand on his knee. "Rafael, we'll figure out what happened to Diego and why once he wakes up. You won't do him any good if you go off half-cocked."

Rafael snorted. "I'm not doing him any good now. Look at him, Vivian. Maybe you don't know what all the bruising and broken bones are a result of, but I've been around this kind of thing most of my life. He wasn't given this good old-fashioned beat down for no reason. Someone was delivering a warning."

"A warning?" She recoiled at the vehemence in his voice. "What kind of warning?"

"The kind that says shut up and take your punishment like a man, or this ass-kicking will be the least of your problems."

Her mind was spinning in circles as she stared at Rafael in dawning horror. "What are you saying?"

"I'm saying the timing of this attack is damn suspicious. Either someone bided his time after Diego got arrested, or all those news reports talking about your firm taking on Diego's case got somebody nervous." Rafael eyed her grimly. "Guess which option I think is the right one?"

"This is about me helping Diego? How can you be so sure of that? Maybe it was just a random thing, like what happened to me the other night."

"Diego knows these streets, and he knows how to protect himself. It would take more than one or two guys to mess him up this much." He looked at Diego and shook his head. "No, this kind of beating is done for a very specific reason. And call me suspicious, but I think whoever did it was trying to convince Diego to roll over and take the fall for a crime he didn't commit. Or else."

RAFAEL HUNG UP his cell phone and stuffed it back in his pocket with a muffled curse. Nothing today was going the way he'd hoped it would, and it was beginning to seriously piss him off.

"Don't worry about anything," he muttered to Diego. "I'll get all this figured out—I promise you that much."

"Hey, what happened?" Vivian asked as she came through the doorway, a cup of coffee in each hand. "You look worse than when I left."

"I just talked to Diego's father. The guy's been useless since his wife died of cancer a few years ago, but I thought knowing that Diego needed him would somehow get him motivated."

She handed him a cup, then sat down in the next chair. "I take it things didn't work out the way you'd hoped."

"Not by a long shot." Rafa glanced at Diego, then lowered his voice—who knew how much the kid could actually hear? The doctor said the drugs had him completely knocked out, but Rafael wasn't taking any chances.

"He basically said that he didn't give a damn about his son, that Diego was a murderer who deserved what he got."

"My God."

"Yeah. That's pretty much what I was thinking."

He'd known when he'd called Diego's father that the old man probably wouldn't be too broken up about what had happened to his son, but he hadn't cared at all. The only thing he'd gotten worked up about at all was making sure Rafael knew he wouldn't be responsible for the hospital bills.

"What am I supposed to tell Diego when he wakes up? That his father didn't care enough about him to ask how he was doing, let alone put down his bottle and come to the hospital?"

"Don't tell him anything unless he asks. Diego's a smart kid—I'm sure he knows where his dad stands."

"I know." Rafael rubbed his hands over his eyes as weariness set in. "It's just that this kid can't catch a break. He's been living in hell for nine weeks, and every time I think we're making some progress, things just get worse. I don't even know what to do now, how to help him."

The thought made Rafa nauseous enough that for a minute he was afraid he was going to puke all over his favorite pair of Doc Martins. Bending over slightly, he braced his hands on his knees and struggled for control.

It took a few seconds, as every instinct he had was screaming at him to find who had done this and tear them apart.

Vivian reached over and squeezed his hand. "You'll figure it all out."

"I don't think—"

"You will." Her voice was soothing, certain. "You're frantic right now, but give it a little time. Things will get sorted out. They always do."

He couldn't help wondering what Vivian's life was like that she could be so optimistic. Nothing in his own had shown him that this would turn out anything but bad. "You don't know that, don't know what a beating like this can do to a body…and a soul."

"I'm sorry." Her face was white, her lush lips compressed into a tight line. "I didn't mean to overstep."

Rafael grimaced. What was it about this woman that had him making an ass of himself in front of her again and again? Sure, her money and status rubbed him the wrong way, but she'd been nothing but kind to Diego.

"You didn't. I'm just prickly."

A little of the tension left her body at his words. "You

have every right to be. This is hard stuff you've got going on right now. Who wouldn't be a little freaked out?"

"Diego's special." He faced the wall behind the youth's bed, unable to look at Vivian. "I mean, all the kids at the center are special in their own way. I've been working with them, watching them grow, for seven years now—ever since I started the place. But every once in a while a kid comes along who just has the whole package. Smart, funny, compassionate.

"Diego has all that and more despite everything that's happened to him. He just needs a little help."

"You're giving him that help."

"I don't know about that. It sure as hell doesn't look like I'm helping."

"Of course it does." She scooted her chair closer, laid a hand just above his knee. "He worships you—I knew that within five minutes of meeting him. And a kid like Diego doesn't give his loyalty to someone who doesn't deserve it."

"Sometimes the world sucks, you know that? It just sucks."

"Yes, it does."

Her quick, heartfelt agreement surprised him, had him turning to look at her. She was closer than he thought, so close that he could smell the sweet, *dulce de leche* smell of her. So close that he could see the silver flecks in her purple eyes.

So close that when she took a deep breath and exhaled slowly, he could feel it.

He couldn't remember the last time he'd let a woman get this close to him for anything other than sex.

Something shifted between them at the thought, and he found himself really looking at Vivian for the first time. She appeared tired, worn-out, even a little frightened.

He didn't like seeing her like that, much preferred it when she was matching him taunt for taunt. Reaching out, he traced a gentle finger over the worry lines between her eyes.

She jumped, drew in a startled breath, but she didn't jerk away, didn't tell him to keep his hands to himself. Suddenly he wanted, very badly, to kiss her.

"Rafael." It was his turn to jump, and he turned to find Marie Lopez, the woman who ran his dining hall, standing at the door.

Pulling away from Vivian, he crossed the room, while wondering what the hell had gotten into him.

"Hey, Marie. I'm glad you came." He leaned down so she could hug him, as she did so many of the kids at the center. She was an older woman, in her late fifties, yet the kids related to her. Loved her, just as she loved them.

"I came as soon as I heard." She clung to him for a second, then went over to the bed and ran a tender hand over Diego's battered face. "How is he?"

"Not good." He told her the details the doctor had relayed to them, watching Marie's face grow sadder and sadder with each revelation.

When he finished his recitation, she cursed roundly and with a no-holds-barred attitude that had Rafael blinking. He couldn't believe the words coming out of her mouth, as she was usually the one at the center demanding that the kids watch what they said.

When she finally paused to take a breath, he said, "Jesus, Marie. Where did you learn to talk like that?"

Her look was disgusted. "Where do you think? I've listened to you and the kids for how long now?"

"Seven years."

"Exactly!"

He smiled gently. "Thanks for coming."

"Where else would I be?" She glanced at Diego. "I'm done with this, Rafael. I'm *so* done with this sense-less violence. What's wrong with these kids today?"

"This wasn't Diego's fault!" Vivian said, her voice indignant as she turned on Marie like an angry she-cat.

The woman didn't back down, simply glared at Vivian and gave as good as she got. "I never said it was. Who are you, anyway? I've never seen you before." Her expression said she wasn't impressed.

Vivian stiffened, her eyes narrowing in a way that surprised him. "I'm—"

"This is Vivian Wentworth. She's Diego's lawyer."

Marie didn't drop her gaze. "Are you any good?" she asked with a sniff of disdain.

"Marie!"

"Yes, I am," Vivian answered. "I'm very good."

"You don't look it."

Rafael felt his jaw tighten in discomfort at Marie's easy dismissal of Vivian, especially since it so closely mirrored his own original reaction. He'd felt justified at the time, but watching the same scene play out again, he couldn't help feeling ashamed of his behavior.

"It's nearly midnight." Marie turned toward him. "You should head back to Helping Hands, shut it down for the night. Shawna and Jake are holding the fort, but they have class in the morning." The two interns were working on their master's degrees in psychology and had been a godsend to the center for the past few months.

"I don't want to leave Diego alone—"

"I'll sit with him tonight. You look exhausted, and mad as hell. Go stretch your legs a little, get some sleep." She glanced behind her at Diego. "We'll see you in the morning."

Before he knew exactly what had happened, Rafael found himself outside of the hospital, staring at his bike. Vivian was beside him and, judging from her face, she was as exhausted as he felt. "Do you want me to drop you home?"

"My car's at the center."

"Oh, yeah, that's right." He handed her her helmet. "Let's go then."

He took it slow, nothing like the headlong rush to the hospital a few hours earlier. But with every mile that passed, he grew more and more aware of Vivian's soft breasts pressed against his back. They'd rushed out of the center without their coats, and the temperature had steadily dropped in the time they'd been at the hospital. She was shivering a little, and when he took a corner a little faster than he should have, she tightened her arms around him until they were pressed tightly together.

Her could feel her nipples through the thin silk of her shirt, the thin cotton of his, and couldn't help the rush of blood to his dick. His groan was lost in the wind rushing by them, and he tried to tell himself his reaction was just stress. Just worry. That it was everything and anything but the fact that he enjoyed the feel of Vivian's arms around him.

Yet he continued to take the curves a little too fast, sped up and weaved around a few cars just to feel her arms tighten around his waist. To feel her press herself more firmly against him.

Goddamn it, what was with him and rich girls with innocent eyes and blackened hearts? God knew after what had happened with Jacquelyn he should have been cured of the obsession. Hell, before Vivian came along he would have sworn he was completely inoculated. And yet here he was, totally turned on and desperate to bury himself inside Vivian, even though he didn't want to trust her—or anyone else who wasn't family.

But the fact of the matter was, after their conversation in Diego's room, everything inside of him was screaming that she was different. That she was *better.* Of course, that's what he'd thought about Jacquelyn all those years before, and the only thing trusting her had gotten him was five years behind bars for a rape that had never happened.

The years he'd spent in prison had broken his mama's heart—and had nearly broken him as well. Every time his parents or siblings visited him, it had grown harder and harder to look them in the eye, until he'd started telling them not to come at all. Not surprisingly, they hadn't listened, had kept coming every week for five long years.

Despite Jacquelyn's crazy accusations—designed to get her back in her father's good graces after he'd caught her sleeping with the help—his family had believed him when he said he was innocent. When he'd finally got out of prison, he'd pledged to himself that he'd never get himself, or his family, stuck in that kind of nightmare again.

Yet here he was, lusting after exactly the wrong kind of woman. Again. Was he ever going to learn?

Rafael gunned the bike's engine harder than necessary as he whipped into the alley behind the center. Vivian jumped a little behind him, and he ended up feeling like a heel. Just because he'd obviously lost his mind didn't mean he needed to take it out on her.

Pulling the bike to a stop beside the back door of Helping Hands, he waited for her to unpeel herself from around him before he climbed off the bike. "Come on," he said, heading inside without glancing her way. "I'll let you into my office to get your briefcase and coat."

"Thanks."

As they walked inside, he did his best to pretend she wasn't there. He knew himself too well, knew that the rage and sorrow and desperation he felt were a bad combination, and if he wasn't careful he was going to end up doing something stupid. Like kissing Vivian when he should be putting as much distance between the two of them as possible.

Rafael gritted his teeth as he neared his office. She was so close he could actually feel her behind him, her breath coming in soft little pulses against his shoulder.

But it was just the stress, the worry over Diego that was making him nearly desperate for the feel of her in his arms. So what if he was attracted to her—he wasn't an animal. He could handle it, ignore it. He sure as hell didn't have to do anything about it. No matter how good she smelled.

Or looked.

Or sounded.

He pushed open the door to his office and then stepped out of the way so she could pass, careful to stand far enough away that she didn't have to touch him as she crossed the threshold. There was no sense in tempting fate, no matter how strong he thought his control was.

She reappeared a few seconds later, with her brief-case in one hand and her coat in the other. "I'll call you tomorrow—to see how Diego is."

He nodded, then glanced away, because what he really wanted to do was pull her into his arms and feel her warm, lush body pressed against his own. "Sure."

"I want you to contact me as soon as he wakes up," she continued, completely oblivious to the sudden need he was trying so hard to hide. "I don't want him questioned by the police unless we're both there."

"All right."

"I'm serious, Rafael. He can't talk to them unless I'm present. I know he's the victim and they'll tell you they only want to find out who did this to him, but I'm telling *you* it's a load of crap. I've been involved with enough domestic violence cases to know how easy it is to blame the victim."

"I got it." He made the mistake of looking at her, and his need for her kicked up another notch—or five.

Clenching his fists, fighting the ridiculous attraction for all it was worth, he headed toward the door at a near run. "As soon as the police show up, I'll call you," he promised.

"Good. And—"

"And don't let them anywhere near Diego until you get there."

She studied him for a moment, her eyes moving over him as if she was searching for something specific. He tried to keep the hard-ass look in place, not wanting her to know how much he desired her.

But she didn't say anything else, simply nodded and waggled her fingers in a little wave before turning away and heading toward her car.

He wanted to call her back, wanted to ask her to stay and just talk to him for a while. Wanted more than anything to pull her into his arms and kiss her until she made him forget what a truly terrible, messed-up day it had been.

Which was exactly why he let her go.

CHAPTER SIX

VIVIAN CLIMBED INTO HER car with a sigh, but she didn't start it right away, choosing instead to rest her head on the steering wheel as her confused emotions ran rampant.

She was getting in too deep with Diego and with Rafael, caring too much about both of them, and she needed to put on the brakes. Diego was a client, she reminded herself, albeit a young one in desperate need of help. But still *just* a client. She needed to step back, be objective, not hurt so badly for him. If she didn't, she wouldn't be much use as his lawyer.

Reason before emotion. The words of her favorite law school professor came back to her. *You can feel as much compassion for a client as you want—after the trial— but keep it out of the courtroom, otherwise you're doing both of you a disservice.*

It was a rule she'd lived by up until now. No matter how angry she was over what had happened to her pro bono clients, she kept her emotions out of it, at least until after they'd won in court.

But she couldn't do that with Diego when he was so lost and in so much trouble. Vivian's sister had died years before—confused and alone—because no one had helped her when she needed it. Though the situations were different—Merry had been the victim, not the accused—something about Diego reminded her of her older sister. Like Merry, he was innocent, without guile, and like Merry, he was being punished for it.

Vivian had been too young to save her sister from her abusive marriage, but she wasn't a kid anymore. She would not see Diego suffer any more than he already had simply because the people in control didn't believe him. She wouldn't turn her back on him the way her parents had turned their backs on Merry.

She could do this, she told herself. Help Diego and find a way to regain her objectivity. Even as she told herself it was possible, a picture of Diego bruised and battered and broken rose in her mind, and she knew, for better or worse, that she wasn't going to be stepping back anytime soon.

If she ended up getting hurt because she couldn't keep her distance, then that was nobody's business but hers. She'd find a way to deal with it.

As for Rafael… She banged her head on the steering wheel a couple of times. What was wrong with her that she was so attracted to him? A few kind words in a hospital room and suddenly she was willing to forget how ugly he'd been to her? She didn't trust him and he sure as hell didn't trust her, yet all she'd been able to think of on the ride home was cuddling as close to him as possible. She'd wanted to crawl around him, surround him, take away the pain she could feel in every tense muscle and see in every line on his face. It was ridiculous. He made her nervous—he was too big, too strong, too dominant for her. He wanted to control everything, when she was used to being the one in control.

Admittedly, after watching her sister suffer at the hands of her smooth, handsome, well-built husband, Vivian was a lot more cautious than most women. She liked to play it safe, and though Rafael was a lot of things—sexy, smart, strangely compelling—he was not the least bit safe.

The vulnerability he made her feel was proof of that. Lessons had started early at her house and she'd spent nearly thirty years learning how dangerous it was to leave herself emotionally exposed to someone else. There was no way she was going to voluntarily let Rafael in and hope he didn't hurt her.

Diego was a kid who couldn't help himself, so she didn't have a choice there. But Rafael was another story altogether and there was no way she could afford to go there.

Her decision didn't stop her libido from standing up and taking notice—something it hadn't done in quite a while. Maybe it was his utter lack of interest in her appearance. Or his prickly attitude and bad-ass looks that hid a heart that was much softer than he liked to admit. Or maybe—

Who cared what it was that attracted her? The point was she needed to get over it, to put it behind her so she could have some peace of mind. Barring that, she needed to ignore it so that she could do her job. Getting involved with her client's guardian was an obvious conflict of interest.

But she could still see how he'd looked before she left—bereft, lonely, a little out of his depth. Kind of how she felt right now. No, she thought with a sigh, that was exactly how she felt.

Suddenly, all her arguments didn't matter. She fumbled with the door handle, climbed out of the car and ran across the alley to the center as the frigid wind whipped around her. She didn't know what she was expecting to happen, only that she didn't want to go home to her lonely apartment.

Slipping through the still unlocked door, she started down the dim hallway, unsure of where to begin looking for him. A quick glance in his office revealed that it was empty, and she began to head upstairs to see if he was in one of the classrooms he and Diego and been renovating.

At the last minute, though, she changed her mind and padded into the big rec room at the front of the center. As soon as she entered, she spotted him sitting on the couch near the brightly decorated Christmas tree. The lights were still on, flashing and sparkling in all their multicolored glory. They looked incongruous playing over Rafael's dark hair and clothes as he sat staring at the floor, elbows on knees, hands buried in his too-long hair. As if none of the joy in the room had managed to touch him.

"What are you still doing here?" He didn't glance up.

"I wanted to make sure you were okay."

"Why wouldn't I be?"

"This thing with Diego—it would shake up anyone."

"It's late, Vivian. Go home."

"I'm planning to. I want…"

"What do you want?" He did look at her then, his black eyes gleaming in the soft light. "What the hell do you want from me?"

A part of her wanted to scramble away from all that furious male aggression, but she refused to back down so easily. If he needed to lash out at her to prove he still had control of his life, then she was more than strong enough to take it.

"I don't know." She whispered the words because they were true. And because she didn't know what else to say.

"That's a cop-out."

"It's the truth." She knelt and placed her hands over his.

"I don't think so." He pulled his hands from hers, only to wrap them around her elbows. Then he dragged her up until her face was only inches from his own. "I think you knew exactly what you wanted when you came back in here." He tugged her a little closer. "It's the same thing I've wanted since I sat next to you in that hospital room."

Vivian's heart pounded a little harder, a little faster, but she didn't pull away. Rafael was right. She did want him—enough to chance being vulnerable, at least for a little while.

Yet he didn't kiss her as she expected him to. Instead, he held her there for long seconds, suspended, her lips a few scant inches from his mouth. He was so close that she could smell the peppermint on his breath, could almost hear the wild pounding of his heart, a perfect match for the sudden craziness of her own.

"Rafael." It was a whimper, a protest, an invitation, a plea.

And still he didn't kiss her.

He closed those eyes and rested his forehead lightly against her own. They stayed that way for a while, drawing comfort from each other.

"I want to kiss you." He whispered the words. "I need to taste you, to feel your lips beneath mine and know that you want me as much as I want you."

She held her breath, waited for his kiss like she'd never waited for anything in her life.

And waited.

"Rafael?" Confused, she let her eyelids flutter open, and found him watching her.

"Say yes." His voice was ragged, his breathing more so.

"Yes." She sighed. "Yes, yes, yes."

He smiled at that—a curve of his lips that was more dangerous, and more delicious, than anything she'd ever seen. Soon his hands were sliding up her arms, over her shoulders, his fingers gliding over her neck and up until he cupped her face in his huge, work-worn palms.

Her eyelids felt heavy, but she forced them to stay open so she didn't miss one second of the most exciting, sensual experience of her life.

Then he was leaning forward, closing the small gap between them and placing his lips reverently on hers.

For one second, his kiss was soft, sweet, his lips as gentle as a butterfly's wings. But then it was as if a giant floodgate had opened inside of him and his emotions and passions came pouring out.

He captured her mouth with his own, using his lips and tongue and teeth to brand her in a way she wouldn't soon forget.

And it was good, better than good. It was magnificent. He tasted like moonlight and the richest, darkest chocolate. Wild and exotic, like every dream she'd ever had but had never known to look for.

He nipped at her lower lip and she moaned, opening to him without a qualm, knowing only that she wanted more of him, that she wanted everything he could give her and more.

She moved her mouth against his, then ran her tongue over his full lower lip and savored the luxurious taste of him.

He groaned at the first touch of her tongue, and she sucked the harsh sound into her mouth to ease the wholly unfamiliar ache whipping through her.

Was this what she'd been missing? she wondered vaguely, as Rafael took the kiss even deeper. This fire that licked through her veins and made her burn for more? For everything?

She tightened her arms around his neck, pressed her body more firmly against his and opened herself to whatever he wanted to give her. She needed him, needed *this,* in a way she'd never before imagined.

He took it slow, torturously slow. Kissed the corners of her mouth before tracing his tongue over her upper lip and lingering at the indention there.

"Rafael," she gasped, wanting more of this incredible feeling that chased all the fears and worries and pain from her head.

"I've got you, Vivian." He pulled her closer, cradled her in his arms as he did crazy, wild things to her mouth. She reveled in each nibble and lick that stoked the flames inside of her.

When he broke away she cried out, tried to hold him

to her, but he refused to stay. Instead, he trailed his lips over her cheek and up to her forehead, lingering at her temple for a moment before kissing his way back down to the curve of her jaw.

How could he be so calm, she wondered vaguely, while she was melting from the inside out? How could he control himself so well, when all she could think of was crawling inside him and begging him to finish what he'd started?

"Rafael." His name burst from her as her hands tangled in the silky length of his hair, and he groaned. The sound sent shivers down her spine, and Vivian sighed. It was too much, too soon, but at this particular moment she didn't care. All she could think of, all she could imagine, was him.

"Wait." He pulled away, panting heavily. "We can't do this."

"What's wrong?" His sudden withdrawal left her feeling exposed.

"I want—"

Before he could finish, a loud crash sounded behind her and she jerked, startled. But Rafael was already moving, climbing off the couch as he thrust her behind him.

"Stay here!" he growled, and then he was running out the front door while she stared aghast at the hole in the center of the huge glass picture window that faced the street. And the brick that had just crashed through it.

CHAPTER SEVEN

RAFAEL RAN DOWN Ellis Street as fast as he could, trying to get close enough to read the license plate on the car weaving through the night. Even after it careened around the corner of Main, he kept running, hoping that something, anything, would happen to slow them down. He just needed a minute to catch up….

He turned the corner and then stopped abruptly, completely disgusted. The street was deserted, the car—and the kids who had thrown the brick—gone as if they had never existed.

Swearing viciously, he jogged back to the center. It was just registering that he'd left Vivian alone there, with a hole the size of a small person in the front window. Though logic told him she was fine, he ran faster, determined to make sure she *was* all right.

He focused on that—and on who would vandalize the center—as he ran the half mile back. Anything to keep his mind off the spectacular kiss he and Vivian had shared. He hadn't planned on kissing her, had told himself to stay as far from her as he could get. But she'd smelled so good, and had sounded so sweet when she'd asked him if he was all right, that he hadn't been able to resist.

Once his lips had touched hers, his objections hadn't seemed to matter, and he'd nearly eaten her alive. Talk about smooth—not. Add the brick through the window to the less-than-suave way he'd jumped her bones, and he figured it would be a miracle if she hadn't run screaming to her car.

Back to her midnight-blue BMW. He hadn't noticed it when they'd run to the hospital, but he'd sure as hell noticed it when they'd come back. Thousand-dollar suits, hundred-thousand-dollar cars—she was so far out of his league it was amazing they were on the same playing field.

He'd had no business kissing her when she was Diego's lawyer. Their lives were too different, and the damn brick just underscored that point. He was pretty sure nothing like this would have happened to her in that upscale apartment building she lived in.

When he got back to Helping Hands, Vivian was still there, standing over the brick and broken glass, the phone in her hand. "The police are on their way," she said softly to him, before going back to her conversation with who he assumed was the 911 operator.

He started to tell her to never mind, that such things had happened before when he'd first opened the teen center, and the cops had never done anything about it at the time. But then he saw the bright red writing on the large brick and the resignation that had been running through his veins exploded into anger.

Tell the bitch to back off. Or else we will.

"What the hell?" He stooped to pick up the filthy,

offensive thing, but Vivian stopped him with a hand on his shoulder.

"Don't do that. You'll compromise any evidence there might be."

Evidence? Someone had just threatened her and she was worried about evidence? He knew it was the lawyer talking, but still. All he could think of was burning the whole damn world until he found whoever had threatened his woman.

Whoa—the thought stopped him in his tracks, and Rafael started backing away from it almost before it was fully formed in his head. What was he, insane? One kiss, one mistake, did not make her *his* anything, which was a damn good thing. There was no way he was going to fall for a lawyer from the fancy side of the tracks. No way he'd ever put himself—or his family—through that again.

"When are the cops going to be here?" He thrust his hands into his pockets and gave the mess in the middle of the rec room a wide berth.

Who was doing this? he wondered. And why? Was it someone who was angry at Diego for killing Esme, or someone who knew he hadn't, but wanted him to take the blame? Or was there a third possibility he hadn't yet considered?

All he knew was that since the news broke that Vivian was defending Diego, things had gotten out of control. Unless he figured out who was doing this, he had a sick feeling the problems would just get worse.

Vivian hung up the phone with a quiet thank-you, then turned to him. "They gave an ETA of half an hour, but you know how these things go."

"Yeah. We'll be lucky if they make it in two hours."

"Probably."

She shivered as a particularly frigid gust of wind blew in through the broken window.

"Come on. Let's go into the kitchen. It'll be warmer in there." He headed toward the back, not waiting to see if she would follow. A guy who got too dependent on a woman like her was asking for more than trouble. He was asking for disaster.

"Are you hungry?" he queried when he heard her enter the kitchen behind him. "There are always leftovers in the fridge."

He walked over to the pantry, got out the coffee and a filter.

"Yeah, actually, I am. Lunch was a long time ago." She opened the fridge. "Wow, you weren't kidding. There's all kinds of stuff in here."

"We feed a lot of kids every day—not necessarily the ones who hang out here, but the ones who have no place else to go." It still bothered him that he hadn't yet been able to turn the center into a full-scale shelter, so that they could take in kids for the night who had no place to crash.

Someday, he promised himself, as he poured water into the coffeemaker. Someday he'd be able to save those kids who couldn't save themselves.

"That's amazing—I hadn't realized you guys did that every day."

He shook his head. "It's not amazing. It's sad that that's all I can do, sad that there's always enough money for guns and drugs and never enough to take care of our children."

"Still," she said, pulling out a tray of enchiladas, followed by a salad. "It's really impressive. Especially in this neighborhood, where there's so much suffering."

"I think there's probably some chicken in there from the other night," he said. "In case you don't want the enchiladas."

"Are you kidding?" She grinned at him, and it was a real smile, despite the lines of strain around her eyes. "I love enchiladas. Especially cheese ones."

"That surprises me."

"Does it?" she asked, as she licked red sauce off her fingers. "Why?"

"I don't know. They seem kind of messy for you." He gestured to her fancy suit.

The look she shot him was oddly disappointed. "I think you have me confused with my mother. I live on takeout, preferably Chinese and Mexican."

The microwave dinged, and she slipped a couple enchiladas onto each of their plates, then settled on one of the red, plastic-covered bar stools. "Aren't you going to join me?"

He studied her, captivated by the impatient challenge in her eyes. Her hair, which had been pulled into some kind of sophisticated twist when she'd shown up six hours before, was now tumbling free of the hairpins. It was a really sexy look for her and it turned him on despite the circumstances.

Tell the bitch to back off.

The words on the brick ran through his mind yet again, and he shoved down his attraction. He needed to figure out what the hell was going on.

"What have you done in the last few days?" he demanded as he slid onto the bar stool to her left.

"I don't know what you mean."

"Look, don't play games with—" He stopped as Vivian stared at her enchiladas in amazement.

"This is fabulous." She shoveled another bite into her mouth, took her time savoring it. "I mean seriously fabulous," she repeated, after swallowing.

"Marie's a great cook." Watching Vivian eat was the first real enjoyment he'd had in a while, Rafa realized.

"Marie made this?" she asked. "That tough, no-nonsense woman from the hospital? She didn't look like the nurturing type."

"She's in charge of the dinner program, among other things."

"You are one lucky man."

"You should taste her lasagna. It's enough to make a grown woman cry."

"Well, you'll have to call me the next time lasagna night rolls around. I'll be here with bells on."

As the reality of her words set in, the levity went out of the moment, and Rafael watched in consternation as Vivian's smile faded. He wanted to say something to bring it back, but Diego's situation was weighing heavily on him.

"So." She cleared her throat as she crossed to the fridge and pulled out two bottles of water. "Are we going to talk about that brick and what it means?"

He circled back to his original topic. "Why don't we talk about what you've been doing this week first?"

"I've been doing my job. I've looked at all the evidence the D.A.'s office has, and made squabbling noises about some of it. Filed a motion to get Diego's trial moved to juvenile court." She took a sip of water. "Got the paralegals started on drafting a motion to suppress anything and everything Diego said during questioning, as he was grilled without a parent, guardian or lawyer present. We won't need it until after the judge decides where to have Diego's trial, but I want it to be ready."

"Why move to suppress the questioning? He never admitted to anything."

"That's not the point. I want it on record that from the very beginning the cops have been cutting corners and doing things illegally. A jury would never hear about it, but a juvenile court judge sure as hell will, and most likely, won't be impressed." She said the last with a look that could have boiled water.

Why had Rafael thought this woman didn't know how to do her job? She'd been on the case four days and already she'd done more than the P.D. who had been on it for nine weeks. Not for the first time, he cursed Jacquelyn and what she'd done to him, not just the baseless accusations that had landed him in prison, but the prejudice he now wore like a second skin.

Normally it didn't bother him, as he considered his dislike of rich people more than justified considering how fast most of his employers had turned on him once he'd been arrested. But misjudging Vivian made him uncomfortable. It had him wondering what other assumptions he'd made about her that might not be true.

Refusing to go down that road, at least for now, Rafael pulled his mind back to the issue at hand. "How much of this is common knowledge? I know the press knows some of it—they've been calling the center, and yesterday I saw an article that mentioned your involvement."

"I don't know how much the press knows. They're obviously aware that my law firm is representing Diego—that paperwork got filed Tuesday morning, after I met with Diego, so by now it's a matter of public record. But the rest…who knows what they've managed to dig up? Whatever it is, I'm sure we'll see it on the six o'clock news tomorrow—if it hasn't already run."

"And that's it? You haven't done anything else?"

"Pretty much. Oh, this morning I met with the detectives who investigated Diego's case."

"Turner and Barnes?"

"Yeah. They weren't particularly impressed with me."

"I bet not." His stomach clenched nervously. "What did you think of them?"

She shrugged. "I didn't particularly like them—especially Turner."

"Yeah, that was my reaction. They seemed more concerned with closing the case than finding Esme's true killer. Plus, they don't exactly have the best reputation in the Tenderloin, if you know what I mean."

"That's what I wanted to know, actually. I hired an investigator to look into them today."

He froze. "Shit, Vivian, are you kidding me? No wonder they're throwing bricks through my window."

"You don't actually think two police officers did that?"

"No, but that doesn't mean they didn't get someone to do it for them."

"They don't even know I did it—"

"Don't bet on that. If some guy starts asking questions about them, don't you think someone would have tipped them off? Another cop? A neighbor? For all its violence, the Tenderloin is a really tight-knit area—everyone knows everybody else's business. Especially the bad stuff."

"But Diego was beat up before I met with the cops!"

"I know, but his assault fits in here somehow. I'd bet a hundred bucks it's all tied together. We just don't know how."

"You make this sound like a conspiracy, Rafael. Why? Diego's not that important in the grand scheme of things."

"Yeah, but maybe whoever killed Esme *is*. If her death was drug related, maybe the cops are being paid off to keep the real perp out of jail. God knows we've got our share of crooked cops and politicians around here." Rafael shook his head. "I don't know what's going on, but something definitely isn't right."

"That's crazy!"

He laughed. "I'm not sure where you think you are, Vivian, but life down here is more than crazy for a lot of these kids. It's downright cruel."

"I know that, Rafael. I do," she insisted when he raised an eyebrow. "But how am I supposed to do my job if I'm worried about Diego getting killed? Or you?"

"You *don't* worry about it. That's my job. You need to concentrate on getting Diego a fair shot. That's why I went after your law firm to begin with."

"Even if it gets him killed?"

"I won't let it." Now that he knew there was a

problem, there was no way one of those bastards was getting within five miles of Diego. But Vivian still didn't look convinced.

"Vivian, spending twenty-five years of his life in a cage for a murder he didn't commit is going to hurt Diego more than a few bruises will."

"It's more than a few bruises, Rafael. He nearly died." She pushed away from the table and started pacing the kitchen in obvious frustration. Her back was to him and he watched her walk, admired the graceful easiness of her movements.

"I know that. And believe me, it's killing me that I didn't protect him. But you have to trust me—I *won't* let it happen again. Besides, if you ask him, he'll tell you they're all worth it if it means he has a shot at being free."

"How do you know that?" she demanded, pacing back again. "He's in a coma. Half-dead. How can you possibly know what he's thinking?"

"Because I've been where he is. And I would have given anything, taken any beating, if someone had stepped forward and helped me when I was too stupid to figure out that I couldn't help myself. If they had, maybe I wouldn't have wasted five years of my life in prison."

EVERYTHING CEASED in the wake of Rafael's revelation. Her heart stopped beating, and even her brain seemed to freeze before her body's survival instinct kicked in.

"You've been to prison?" Her voice was reed thin. "For what?"

He eyed her grimly, and even before he opened his mouth she knew it was going to be bad. Really bad.

Bracing herself, she waited for his answer the way a death row inmate waited for execution day.

But for all her preparation, it was still a shock when he tersely answered, "Raping my girlfriend."

The room started to spin, and for the first time in a long while Vivian's legs threatened to go out from under her. Grabbing the counter, she kept herself standing through sheer force of will.

Rafael had gone to prison for rape.

She was attracted to a rapist.

She had kissed a rapist.

Her stomach churned at the thought, had her wondering if she was going to puke up Marie's enchiladas all over the spotless kitchen floor.

Trying to regain a semblance of control, Vivian looked wildly around the room, concentrated on the stove, the refrigerator, the pale yellow walls. Looked anywhere and everywhere but at Rafael.

Eventually, though, there was nothing else to stare at, and she reluctantly shifted her gaze back to him. His face was carefully blank, his eyes empty, but his jaw was tense, his lips pressed tightly together as he watched her.

She knew he was waiting for her to say something, but she didn't have a clue *what* to say. For years, she'd seen the result of rape and violence at the battered women's shelters. Worse, she'd seen what it had done to Merry—years of rape and abuse at the hands of her husband had slowly destroyed Vivian's sister until suicide had seemed like her only option.

It had been nine years since Merry had killed herself, but sometimes it felt as if it had just happened. On bad days, Vivian could still see her sister's bruised, battered, bloodied body hanging naked from the ceiling fan.

She almost didn't make it to the trash can in time.

Even as she was throwing up, Vivian was conscious of Rafael halfway across the kitchen. He didn't attempt to come near her, didn't say a word, but she could feel him staring at her, and that shook her even more than getting sick did.

It seemed as though it went on forever—dry heaves racking her body long after her stomach was empty. When it was finally over, she crossed to the sink, rinsed her mouth out with water and tried to figure out what to say.

In the end, she said the only thing that mattered, asked the only question her shocked brain could form. "Did you do it?"

"No." His voice was hoarse, his answer immediate.

"I don't believe you." The words were instinctive.

"Do I look surprised?"

She couldn't even glance at him. "Why?"

"Why didn't they believe me? Or why was I accused?"

She swallowed against the bile that was once again creeping up her throat. "Why did you do it?"

His fist came down hard on the table. "I *didn't*. Her father caught her sneaking back into the house one night. She'd been pretty roughed up. She told him I did it, even though I hadn't seen her since early that morning. When the rape kit came back with two distinct sets of DNA—one of which belonged to her 'public' boyfriend and one which belonged to me—they arrested *me* even though I had never hurt her."

"So why did she accuse you?"

"For kicks? Because she was too embarrassed to tell her father she was seeing one of the gardeners? It was fifteen years ago, during the summer, and I was mowing grass to save up money for my sophomore year of college.

"Or maybe it was because she was a vindictive bitch. I'd told her that morning that I wasn't going to keep sneaking around. If she was so ashamed of me she couldn't introduce me to her parents, then I wanted to break up. She assured me she wanted to be with me, that she would tell her father about us. The next thing I knew, I was being arrested for rape."

Vivian wanted desperately to believe him, but every story she'd ever heard was echoing in her head. The excuses made by the abused, the lies told by the abuser. The details of rapes and beatings and attempted suicides running through her mind like a never-ending montage. And Merry. *Dear God, Merry.*

"I want to believe you."

"So believe me. Or don't." He shrugged. "It's not like it really matters, unless you're going to back out of defending Diego."

"I wouldn't do that."

"So there's no problem then."

"Rafael—"

A loud knock on the front door had her pausing, biting her lip.

"Hey, don't worry about it. I won't." He walked out without another word.

She watched him go, thoughts of their kiss in the front of her mind.

Too late she remembered his tenderness as he kissed

her, his determination to make sure she was okay. His insistence that she say yes before he so much as touched her.

Sinking into the nearest chair, she laid her head on the kitchen table and tried to convince herself that this whole evening had been a nightmare. Too bad it didn't look like she was going to wake up anytime soon.

CHAPTER EIGHT

"DIEGO, COME ON NOW, KID. Enough's enough."

When there was still no response, Rafael sank deeper into his chair as he tried not to lose hope. It had been three days since the doctor had tried to bring Diego out of the coma, and he still hadn't come around.

Rafael was beginning to think he might never make it back.

Dr. Graham had told him that she couldn't find a medical explanation as to why Diego hadn't woken up, since the drugs had been reduced enough that they weren't keeping him out, and the swelling in his brain had receded. Except for the broken bones and slow-to-fade bruises, Diego's body was almost in the same shape it had been before the beating.

Yet he wouldn't wake up. Marie said she thought the kid was too heartbroken to awaken—after all, what did he have to come back to except a murder charge? The idea that she might be right scared the hell out of Rafael, had him trying harder than ever to figure out how to reach the boy.

"Diego, I need you to wake up. Vivian's got a hearing at juvenile court this week. She's trying to get your trial moved out of adult court so you can be tried as a minor. She thinks she's got a chance at it. A good chance.

"The judge even gave her a quick hearing date on account of everything that's happened to you—nice to know the beating wasn't for nothing, right?" Rafa tried for a laugh, but nothing about this godforsaken situation was funny and he ended up sounding like a dying goose.

"Come on, man. You've got to stop this—you're freaking me out. I need you to wake up. We *all* need you to wake up. Marco's been here and Marie, Shawna, Vivian. A bunch of other kids from the center have stopped by. We've all been sitting around waiting and it's getting to be a drag.

"Besides, you need to wake up so you can tell me whose ass I need to kick. Nobody knows who did this to you, and the police aren't looking too hard, if you know what I mean. *You* need to tell me."

He watched Diego carefully, but nothing happened. No eyelid twitch, no hand movement. None of the signs the doctor had said to watch for. It was as if the kid was already gone.

The thought worried Rafael so much that he'd spent the past few days talking about everything and nothing. Telling Diego about his own childhood. Reminiscing about the scared little kid Diego had been when he'd first shown up at the shelter all those years before.

Nothing had worked, and all this quiet time was driving him crazy. Too much time sitting around thinking about what was waiting for Diego when he woke up. Too much time thinking about Vivian and their blowup Thursday night.

Not that there was all that much to think about. He'd told her something he hadn't told anyone in years, and she'd basically called him a rapist. What had he expected, though?

Rafael sighed. Deep down, he'd known exactly what he was doing when he'd blurted out his past. Even standing there, telling himself that it was because he wanted to help her understand Diego's perspective, he'd known the truth. The kiss they'd shared had been too intimate, and he'd needed to push Vivian away, hard. So hard that she didn't come back to him.

Didn't make him remember what it was to feel something for a woman besides desire.

Didn't make him remember what it was to trust someone.

It had been fifteen years since he'd trusted a woman, and the idea of starting now didn't sit easy with him. Especially when that woman's wealth and social status were so similar to the one who had betrayed him in the first place.

Still, part of him had hoped she'd be different, hoped she'd look beyond the obvious. In the end, she'd been just like everyone else who'd decided he was guilty without listening to his side of the story.

I don't believe you.

It had been one of the first things she'd said, and nothing he'd told her afterward had made a bit of difference. She'd already shut him out.

Her reaction should have satisfied him, should have made him happy that he'd been right about her all along. Instead, he was sitting here miserable, worried like hell about Diego and wondering if there was anything he could do about Vivian.

He sat there for one hour, two, as time passed slowly. He should be at the center. He'd been relying on his employees to carry things there since Diego had been beaten, but he couldn't leave Diego alone and unprotected, either. Plus, the press was circling like rabid wolves. Every few hours a different reporter tried to talk his or her way into the ICU unit. So far none had got through, but he figured it was just a matter of time.

So far, he'd been switching shifts every few hours—he and Marie carried the big ones, but both of Rafael's brothers had sat with Diego a few times, as had Rafael's parents. When he'd tried to thank them, they'd laughed him off. Reminded him that families helped each other out. Ever since prison, he'd sometimes had trouble remembering that, though his family never did.

It was just one of the many ways those five years had changed him.

More time passed and he started drifting somewhere between sleep and wakefulness. Which was why the first time he saw Diego's hand move, he thought he'd imagined it. But when it happened a second, then a third time, he grew more alert, started talking in a rush of words, encouraging Diego to make it back.

And when the kid finally opened his eyes, Rafael was standing right over him, grinning like a fool.

"OH, NO, SWEETHEART, don't buy your father that sweater. We're going to Saint Croix for the holiday and it would be much too hot."

"You didn't tell me you were going to Saint Croix." As she refolded the sweater and continued looking around the men's department. Vivian's nerves were stretched to the breaking point. Not that that was unusual. Spending the day with her mother usually had that effect on her.

"Yes, well, it was a sudden decision, but the islands are so much nicer during the holidays than San Francisco. All this dreary rain is so depressing."

"I guess."

"You know, you're welcome to come. I can still arrange for a larger suite. I just assumed you would be too busy."

Meaning her mother wanted her to be too busy. What fun were the islands when you had to hang out with your stick-in-the-mud daughter the whole time?

Vivian shook her head. It was just like Lillian to make plans for Christmas that didn't include her only child. Forget that Christmas was supposed to be for families. Sunshine was so much more important than togetherness, especially if there was no one around to impress.

"How about this?" she asked, holding up the most obnoxious Hawaiian shirt she could find. "Maybe Dad could wear it on the golf course?"

The pinched look on her mother's face said it all.

"Okay, Mom." Figuring they'd be there all day if she didn't ask, she finally bit the bullet. "What do you suggest I get Dad for Christmas?"

"I'm so glad you asked, darling. Actually, he's been wanting a new set of golf clubs. While we're in the islands, I'm having the gardener rip up the back corner of the yard and put in a putting green for him. It won't be as big as the one at the club, of course, but it'll be a nice place for him to practice."

"You're getting Dad a putting green for Christmas?"

Her mother shrugged delicately. "He has almost everything else."

It was hard to argue with that logic, so she didn't even try. "If you wanted me to buy him golf clubs, why did we bother coming here?"

"Well, I didn't want you to feel you had to get him golf clubs. It's your decision, after all."

Sure it was. Vivian rolled her eyes behind her mother's back. Everything was her decision—as long as she made the choice her mother wanted her to. It was only when she made a different one that all bets were off.

Glancing at her watch, she breathed a sigh of relief. One more hour and she could make her excuses to get out of this mother-daughter bonding day from hell. The police were due at Diego's hospital room at three o'clock and she wanted to leave in plenty of time to beat them there. Especially as she wasn't sure that Rafael remembered her instructions to keep the police out until she got there.

It had been five days since he'd kissed her, five days since he'd told her he'd gone to jail for rape.

Five days since she'd called him a liar and he'd walked away from her without a backward glance.

He had only spoken to her twice since then—when she'd cornered him in Diego's hospital room and he couldn't find a way past her. Not that she had gone out of her way to speak to him, either. She didn't know what to say to him, didn't know what she *could* say. Part of her longed to believe him, but a smaller, more cynical part reminded her that most people weren't wrongly arrested.

Of course, it was pretty hard to accept that argument when she was working day and night to defend a boy who had been just so falsely accused.

At least Diego was out of the woods. After spending six days in a coma that should have ended when the doctors stopped administering drugs on day two, he had finally woken up the night before and spoken to Rafael. It was a huge victory when everyone had begun to fear that they would lose him.

"Are you ready for a late lunch?" her mother asked, interrupting her thoughts. "I have salon appointments for us at two-thirty, but I'm sure we can squeeze in a salad and a martini before then."

"I told you, I can't stay that late. I have someplace I need to be at three o'clock."

"That's ridiculous. This is your first day off in months and you're going to spend it working? I won't have it."

"You don't have a choice. My client has to meet with the police and I need to be there."

When her mother continued to watch her with the cold, flat stare of a cobra, Vivian sighed. "I can have a quick lunch—but no salon."

"But, darling, your hair is a disaster." Lillian rubbed a few strands between her fingers. "It's as dry as a desert. You need one of Pierre's hair masques desperately."

"Yes, well, the hair masque will have to wait. Along with the trim and the facial."

"How exactly do you plan to find a man when you go around looking like a ragamuffin all the time? I swear, I'm embarrassed to take you anywhere. The Black-and-White Ball is on New Year's Eve, and you're expected to attend. That's two weeks away. If you don't make appointments now, you'll never get in. You know how it is this time of year. Do you even have a dress?"

"I don't want one."

"Don't want a new dress?" Her mother looked scandalized.

"Don't want a man. Or a new dress." As she said the words Rafael came to mind, but she pushed him right back out. Even if Friday night had never happened, even if she still had no idea he'd been to jail for rape, she wouldn't be interested. He was too dominant for her, too determined to be the one in control. She'd spent most of her life doing what her parents wanted her to do in an effort not to make waves. Now that she was finally her own woman, living the life she'd always wanted, she'd be damned if she'd saddle herself with a man who expected her to jump at his every command.

Besides, as things stood now, she did know he was a convicted rapist, and that was something she didn't think she could ever get past—no matter what he said.

"Vivian, what are you talking about? I swear, I barely know who you are anymore. It's all that work you do at the shelter—it's changing you."

"I certainly hope so." Vivian gently steered her mother toward the first floor.

"And not for the better." Her mother stepped off the escalator and into her favorite part of Saks—the purse department. "What do you think of this one?"

She held up a boring beige bag that looked just like a million others she had in her closet. "It's fine."

"Hmm, well, maybe." Lillian considered it for a second, then put it back. "And don't think I don't know that's where you're running off to this afternoon."

"Where?" Vivian asked, mystified as she tried to follow the conversation.

"That little shelter of yours with all those miserable women. I called your assistant this morning and she said your whole day was free. So if your afternoon appointment isn't related to the firm—"

"You checked with Marcy?"

"Of course I did." She paused over a gray bag, trailed a finger down the leather. "You never tell me anything."

"Well, my appointment does relate to the firm. It's for the pro bono case Richard assigned me."

"Ah, yes. The boy murderer who has you on the news every night." Her mother picked up another bag, black this time. "How is Richard, by the way?"

"Richard's fine. And Diego isn't a murderer."

"Of course he is, dear. You know, we should have him over to the house soon."

"Diego?" She deliberately misunderstood.

"Richard." Her mother's lips twisted in disapproval. "You know how your father likes him."

"I do, yes."

"Of course, his new wife is a bimbo, but I suppose I can endure. For your sake."

"Don't invite him for my sake, Mom. I'm doing fine on my own."

"Don't be ridiculous. Partnerships are made at the

dinner table, darling, not in the office. And since you insist you don't want a husband, I assume you're aiming for a partnership at the firm."

"Maybe."

"Hmm, well then, you definitely need my help."

"And why is that?"

Her mother looked up from the bag she was perusing and pinned Vivian with the look that had been making her squirm since she was two years old. "Because, dear, everyone knows Richard doesn't take on very many pro bono cases, and the ones he does take, he only gives to lawyers he expects to fail. It's his little way of weeding out those lawyers who aren't measuring up."

She smiled. "Now where did you say you wanted to go for lunch?"

CHAPTER NINE

IT WAS OVER AN HOUR LATER before Vivian was able to escape from her mother's clutches, and she was still reeling from the bombshell Lillian had delivered.

Was her mother right? Vivian wondered as she climbed into her car. Was that why the firm took so few pro bono cases? She tried to think of the last one she'd heard about them accepting. It had been a couple years back. A pretty cut-and-dry drunk driving case, if she remembered correctly. She wasn't sure which lawyer had argued it, though. She remembered he'd lost because the evidence had been stacked against him.

Janssen. That was it. Janssen had argued it, she finally realized, as she pulled out of the mall's parking lot. He was still with the firm.

Yeah, but he hadn't made junior partner despite being at Stanley and Baker for fourteen—or maybe it was fifteen—years.

But that didn't mean Richard was doing the same thing to her. She was a good lawyer, had won all but three cases in the years she'd been at the firm. She'd handled some of the top divorces in the city, had brought in a lot of revenue.

Ugh. She hit the steering wheel. This was crazy. When was the last time she'd believed the vitriol her mother spouted? So why was she letting it get to her now? The whole thing was ridiculous.

Yet a little voice in the back of her head that refused to shut up kept asking why a divorce attorney had been assigned a murder trial. It was a question she couldn't answer.

By the time she got to the hospital, her nerves were stretched tight. The fact that she still hadn't hashed things out with Rafael only stressed her out more. Part of her wanted to believe him when he said he was innocent, but another part of her was afraid. Afraid of making the same mistakes so many of the women she worked with made. Afraid of trusting him and getting hurt.

That fear didn't negate the feelings he aroused in her, though. She'd lain awake half the night thinking about the feel of his lips on hers and wondering if any man who asked so sweetly if he could kiss her and held her so tenderly while he did so was really capable of rape.

Taking a few deep breaths, she struggled to get over her frustration and hurt so that she could do her job. After all, Diego was a hell of a lot more important than her mother's careless nastiness or Vivian's problems with Rafael.

But when she got to Diego's hospital room, her frustration exploded into full-blown anger. Though she was ten minutes early, the cops were already there, and Rafael looked less than happy. It only got worse when the one closest to her glanced up and she realized she was looking at Detectives Turner and Barnes, even though they weren't the ones who had caught the case when Diego had been admitted last week.

Ignoring all of them for a moment, she took in Diego's bruised and battered form. If possible, he looked worse awake than he had while asleep, the misery in his eyes somehow making the bruises and broken bones look that much more horrifying.

She went to him, squeezed his uninjured hand. "How are you doing, Diego? You feeling up to this?"

"I think so." His voice was low, his eyes averted.

"All right then. Let's get this show on the road." She sent him what she hoped was a reassuring smile, then pinned the men across the room with the most intimidating look she had in her repertoire.

"Hello, gentleman." She kept her voice cool. "I trust you haven't been here long, as I made it perfectly clear that you were *not* to speak with my client without me present."

"He's the victim, Ms. Wentworth." It was Turner who answered her—as usual. "We just wanted to get a statement."

"Interesting that they sent the detectives who arrested Diego for homicide to get that statement."

"We were the only ones available this afternoon."

"I bet. So I assume you have some questions, Detective Barnes." She deliberately addressed the younger cop. "Let's try to keep it brief, as my client's been victimized enough recently, don't you think?"

"It's not like we're here to beat a confession out of him," Turner blustered.

"Well, that's a good thing, isn't it? As I don't think

there's much left on my client to break." She stared down her nose at the timeworn detective, before glancing at Rafael for the first time.

He nodded to her from his position on the other side of the bed, and she smiled at him before turning away. This was the first time she'd seen him since they'd argued the other night, and the impersonal look he gave her only made her more uncomfortable.

She made sure none of her inner turmoil came out in her voice when she spoke. "All right then, let's get on with this."

"So, Diego, did you get a look at who did this to you?" Barnes asked the first question.

"No. I don't think so."

"You don't think so?" Turner took over.

"It's kind of fuzzy. I remember it being dark."

"But the doctors say you were attacked in the morning—it was light out."

"Your questions sound an awful lot like accusations, Detective Turner," Vivian interjected.

"I was just wondering why he had such a hard time seeing if it was daylight?"

"I think—I think they put a bag over my head. I remember having a hard time breathing, trying to rip something off my face."

"What kind of bag?"

"I don't remember."

"Well, that's convenient, isn't it?"

"Watch yourself, Detective Turner."

"So, how many guys do you think there were?" Barnes again.

"I'm not sure. Three, maybe four."

"Is there anything you are sure of, Diego? Because if so, feel free to speak up anytime."

"My client sustained a serious head injury, Detective Turner. If you would like, I'm sure I could get his doctor in here to discuss memory loss of traumatic events."

"No, I think I get it."

"Are you sure? I can ask when her rounds are."

"I said it's fine."

Vivian glanced at Rafael, then wished she hadn't. His arms were folded across his chest and it appeared he was having a difficult time keeping his mouth shut.

"Shall we move on?"

Turner nodded. "So, where were you when this happened?"

"Close to school. I'd stopped at Mamacita's, picked up a bagel and an apple for breakfast, then I started walking up Leavenworth."

"That's close to where your girlfriend lived, isn't it? Reliving the good old days?"

"That's it!" Vivian snapped furiously. "May I remind you, gentleman, one last time, that my client is the victim here. You're here to find out who attacked him, not to pump him for details on any other cases. And certainly not to taunt him."

"Other cases?" Turner finally exploded. "He killed his pregnant girlfriend! If you ask me, this beat down barely scratches the surface of what he deserves."

"Well, if that's how you feel, perhaps you should send another detective out here to take his statement. I want the people who did this found, and if you won't take the investigation seriously, I'll find someone who will."

"Is that a threat?"

"It wasn't meant to be. Why? Are you afraid of something?"

"Hey, now..." Barnes stepped in. "Let's stay on task."

"Defending Diego *is* my task, Detective Barnes."

"And why is that?" Turner's eyes swept over her in an insulting manner. "What makes a woman like you defend pond scum like this? I'd expect better from you, Ms. Wentworth."

He put an obnoxious emphasis on the *Ms.*, one that, combined with his rude perusal, made her want to forget about playing nice.

"Don't talk to her like that." Rafael spoke up for the first time, his voice more threatening than she had ever heard it, and she could tell instantly that it got the cops' backs up.

"I can handle this, Mr. Cardoza. Please let me do so."

He didn't say another word, but the frown he sent her way said he wasn't happy. Not that she cared. She wasn't particularly impressed with him for jumping to her defense, either.

"Do you have any other questions?" Once again she spoke to Barnes, who was by far the least offensive of the two.

"Definitely."

"Then I suggest you ask them before I lose my patience."

Turner turned back to Diego, a malevolent look on

his face. "Are you sure you were on Leavenworth? You were found three blocks up on Polk."

"That doesn't make any sense. I know I was walking to school."

"Really? You weren't walking down Polk, scoping out the apartments there?"

"Why would I be looking at apartments?"

"I don't know—lots of pretty girls over that way."

"Detective!"

He ignored her. "Maybe you're missing Esme and are looking for a new victim—er, replacement."

"No!"

"Exactly what are you getting at, Detective Turner?" Vivian demanded.

Barnes answered for him. "We talked to some people who said they saw a guy who looked a little like Diego peeping into some windows near the corner of Polk and Turk."

"So we were wondering if maybe this beat down wasn't a result of your little voyeuristic habit?" Turner smirked. "Maybe you looked in the wrong window, pissed off the wrong *brothers*."

The emphasis he put on the last word bothered Vivian, but before she could explore why, Diego cried, "I've never— I wouldn't— That's not true!" He was visibly agitated, grimacing with each expulsion of sound.

"Okay, that's enough. My client's tired, Detectives. We'll have to pick this up another day." Yeah, when hell froze over.

"We have a few more questions—"

"Well, that's a shame, Detective Barnes, because it

doesn't look like they're going to get answered today." Without breaking eye contact with the officer, she handed Diego the button for the morphine drip that was supposed to help him control pain. He took it gratefully and began to press the button. A few moments later he drifted into an uneasy sleep.

"Goodbye, Detectives." She reached into her pocket and pulled out a business card. "And the next time you want to set up an appointment to speak with my client, you'll need to do so through me."

Turner stared at her for long seconds before finally reaching forward and taking the card. His fingers brushed hers, and they were as cold and clammy as his personality. "I'll do that, Ms. Wentworth." He glanced back at the bed. "Your client has a lot to answer for. Expect my call."

Rafael stepped forward then, bristling with aggressiveness. The detectives responded in kind, and Vivian tried to step in before what little cordiality was left went south. "My client is the *victim*," she repeated for what felt like the hundredth time.

"Your *client* is going down," Turner responded. "And taking everyone around him with him. I'd watch yourself, Ms. Wentworth. That weapons charge didn't come out of nowhere. This kid has a nasty habit of taking his temper out on women who can't defend themselves." His eyes cut to Rafael. "But then, he's following in some pretty big footsteps on that front, isn't he?"

The cop's intimation was so obnoxious that she expected to have to hold Rafael back. But when she glanced at him, she realized he'd shut down—had turned completely emotionless at the reference to his prison time.

"We'll be in touch," Turner called from the hallway.

"I'll look forward to it," she answered, keeping her polite, fake smile in place. Inside she felt sick, as if the blow they'd aimed at Rafael had hit her as well.

The second the cops were gone, she turned to him. "Don't listen to them."

But he was already halfway down the hall, walking away from her—and the unspoken accusations that hung in the air between them—as fast as his long legs could carry him.

HE FELT AS IF HE WAS going to explode. As if his brain was on fire and he was going to spontaneously combust right there in the middle of Saint Francis Hospital.

"Rafael, wait," Vivian called, but he didn't slow down. He didn't want to be around her right now, couldn't stand to look in her eyes and see her contempt. And he sure as hell couldn't stand the idea of talking with her about his past again.

He hated people like those cops, men who, at best, cared more about what they thought they knew than they ever would about the truth. Men who were inflexible about seeing the other side of the story.

It was two cops like that who had arrested him without evidence all those years ago, who had railroaded him right into prison, on the words of a vindictive girl, for a crime he hadn't committed.

The fact that these two guys knew about his past—

and had used it against him in front of Vivian—only made him more upset.

"Am I going to have to chase you through this whole damn hospital or are you going to be reasonable?" Her voice echoed down the hallway after him. "Rafael?"

He continued to ignore her, as he headed into the stairwell. Being reasonable wasn't in his bag of tricks for the day. But about halfway down the second set of steps, he stopped dead, realizing that he'd left Diego alone and undefended.

Shit, he was a bigger basket case than he'd thought.

Knowing he had to go back up, he stood there for a minute and tried to compose himself. It didn't work.

Vivian met him on the landing between floors, her eyes dark with unexpected concern.

Feeling more insecure than he liked to admit—not to mention embarrassed as hell that Vivian had seen those cops humiliate him—Rafael used the same defense he'd been using for his entire adult life: a good offense.

"Those guys were assholes. I didn't like what they were saying about you and Diego. So sue me."

"Rafael."

"Vivian." He mimicked her tone.

"We need to work with them."

He laughed sarcastically. "They don't want to work with us—and they never have. They've had it in for Diego from the minute they got him in their sights for Esme's murder. You think it's a coincidence that they got assigned this case?"

"Of course not. But that's the point." She was speaking in a furious whisper, and he had to bend his head to hear her words. She wore flats today instead of her usual sky-scraper heels, which put her mouth about seven inches below his own, and her voice wasn't carrying. "They're looking for an excuse to make as much trouble for Diego as they can. Don't give it to them."

"In case you haven't noticed, they don't need an excuse to make trouble." He bent closer, crowded her a little with his body, knowing it was a bad idea even as he did so, especially after the way she'd responded the last time they'd been alone together.

She stuttered over her answer as his shoulder brushed against hers. It made him wonder if she was afraid—or aroused.

"T-true, but it never pays to antagonize the guys with power."

"I think I know that better than most." He drew a finger gently down her cheek, testing her response.

Her voice trailed off for a second as her breath caught. Aroused then, not afraid. He liked that. "I'm still waiting for the report on them. Maybe there will be something in it we can use to discredit them. Remember, juvenile court is a whole different ball game."

"There's no guarantee Diego's trial will be moved—wait until the press get wind of the hearing. They'll vilify him." Rafa grew bolder, ran the back of his hand down the silky smooth skin of her cheek to her jaw, then rested his palm against her throat.

"It's on the juvenile docket, so the press won't find out until it's too late. Those names are kept confidential. You know that."

"I wish I had your faith." Her neck was so slender that

his fingers and thumb were only inches away from meeting at the back.

Her heartbeat went crazy—he could feel her pulse pounding rapidly beneath his hand. But she didn't tell him to stop, didn't pull away, didn't do anything but take a few shallow breaths and let him touch her.

His fingers curled and he stroked the fragile column of her throat again and again, transfixed by the differences between them. She was so finely built, so delicate, her skin as pale and pampered as a doll's. His hands were huge in contrast, callused from years of gardening and fixing things around the center.

And yet there was something seductive—something erotic—about the picture they made together. Her so light, him so dark. Her so fragile, him so strong. But as she looked at him without flinching, those fierce warrior eyes all but daring him to do something, he couldn't help wondering which one of them was really the strongest.

"People have already connected the dots, Vivian." He kept his voice low, not wanting anyone to hear their conversation, not wanting anyone to interrupt. "They've just made the wrong picture."

"So we'll change the picture. Once we get to juvenile court, I'm going after the evidence. No way will they ever get Diego's dismissed weapons charge admitted, so the pattern for means is gone. Motive and opportunity are already really shaky. I can do this."

"You can't, sweetheart. The picture's written in indelible ink and the only chance we've really got is if we give them a whole new picture, one they'll like even more than what they've currently got."

He crowded her a little more until her legs tangled

with his and she was leaning back against the wall, completely open to him. "What do—what do you mean by that?"

"I mean, we need to find out who really killed Esme. A cop friend of mine has already spent some time poking around the neighborhood with me, but it's been hard going, since I've been dividing my time between Diego and the center. Now that he's better, it should get easier."

"What do you think you're going to find?"

"Somebody saw something, Vivian. The neighborhood is filled with witnesses—I just need to find the right one."

He pressed a glancing kiss to the corner of her mouth, reveling in the shiver that she couldn't hide. He did it a second time, then a third, unwilling to stop unless she stopped him. She tasted so damn good and for the moment that was enough. He would make it be enough, because there was no way the two of them could work in the long run. The ex-con and the lawyer sounded just as absurd as the rich girl and the boy from the wrong side of the tracks. But when he held her, none of that seemed to matter. At this point he was more than willing to take whatever he could and let the future take care of itself. It always did.

He moved so that his cupped hands slid to the back of her head and he brought her forward, just a little, until her lips met his.

"Rafael," she sighed.

"Let me kiss you. Just a kiss. I promise, " he answered, sipping from her mouth. God, she was sweet—sweeter than any candy he'd ever had. More delicious than anything he'd ever tasted.

"Just one kiss," he said again, and when she made no move to pull away, he covered her lips with his own.

Because he wanted to devour, he forced himself to keep it light. Because he wanted to take, he concentrated on giving. And because he wanted her more than all the other women he'd had in his life combined, he clamped down on the need that was all but consuming him. He didn't want to scare her away; with his past, he had to be careful.

Shifting angles slightly, he ran his tongue over her lower lip. Kept the pressure light as he toyed with her mouth, explored all the angles, learned about her in a way he hadn't been able to the other night. Then, he'd been too wrapped up in the thrill of it, the passion that burned between them like lightning. But today, now, he wanted to get to know her, to understand the subtle flavors of her personality as much—or more—than he wanted to know the taste of her mouth.

But she moaned deep in her throat, tangling her legs with his as she pressed herself against him. He was lost in the unique flavors of her, in the overwhelming feel of her, in the open, honest touch of her tongue against his own.

His hands burrowed more deeply in her hair and he did what he'd sworn he wouldn't—swooped in and took everything she had to give. And demanded more.

She gave it to him, her hands tugging him closer until her breasts were pillowed against his chest, her pelvis cradled by his own. His mouth raced down the silky curve of her jaw.

"Diego," she reminded him as she tilted her head back to give him better access to her throat. "He's alone."

With a groan, Rafael pulled away and went about the painful process of shutting his body down.

Nice job, he told himself. Nothing like promising a

simple kiss and then all but mauling a woman in a hospital stairwell before he'd ever taken her on a date. Cursing himself and the attraction that wouldn't let him leave her alone despite knowing exactly how bad she was for him, Rafael started when Vivian stood on tiptoe to deliver one quick peck to his mouth.

As he looked at her, desire slammed through him all over again. She looked as if she'd been well and truly kissed—her mouth swollen, her makeup smudged, her red hair messed up from his fingers.

Shoving his hands in his pockets, he backed away a little. "You need to fix your hair or the whole floor will know what we've been doing."

"Oh, of course." She ran a hand over the rioting ringlets and did her best to get them under control. "Is that better?"

"I want to see you again." Her gaze jumped to his. "I mean away from this, away from Diego's case. I want to see you," he repeated.

Even as he said the words, he expected her to turn him down. Yeah, they were attracted to each other, but how many women like her really wanted to date a convicted rapist, innocent or not?

But she simply nodded, and said, "Okay."

Feeling like an idiot, knowing he'd regret it as soon as he was away from her and the incredible power she exerted over him, he said, "It's my brother's fortieth birthday on Thursday. We're having a party for him at my parents' restaurant—nothing fancy, just some family and friends. Do you want to go?"

Jesus, he hadn't felt like this big of a moron since

he'd asked his first girl out in junior high, but then, that was the last time a woman's answer had meant this much to him. He was risking everything by asking her out— especially to a party with his family. What were they going to say when they saw him with another girl like Jacquelyn? What was he going to tell them—that she was different? That, for better or worse, she made him feel again?

"I'd love to come. What time?"

"I'll pick you up at six-thirty. Will that give you enough time to get home and changed?"

"I'll make sure of it. Thanks for asking." She smiled, but he searched her face for signs of discomfort. He didn't find any, which could mean that she really was okay with going on a date with him—or that she was a better actress than he'd thought.

The fact that the latter seemed much more likely put a crimp on the satisfaction her agreement had made him feel.

"VIVIAN, WHAT ARE YOU doing here?"

Vivian's heart sank late the next afternoon as she saw her father standing in the middle of his favorite golf shop. She'd been planning on using the early court dismissal to finish her Christmas shopping, and had stopped here to pick up a new set of clubs for her dad. Obviously that wasn't going to happen now.

"Oh, I had a few minutes and thought I'd stop by and check out what was new. The last time I played golf, my father beat the pants off me."

"He did at that." Her dad leaned down and gave her a brief kiss on the cheek, his silver hair gleaming in the store's spotlights. "Is there anything special you're looking for?"

"Something to make me a better golfer."

His laugh was the same smooth, cultured one she remembered from her childhood. "Only practice will do that. Maybe if you slowed down a little on the pro bono work…" He eyed her meaningfully.

"Caught this morning's broadcast, did you?"

"I think the whole city caught that broadcast. 'Baby Killer Out of Coma, His Attorney at His Side.' Seriously, Vivian. Is this the case you want to sink your career on?"

"I don't think it's going to sink my career, Dad. I'm determined to get Diego exonerated."

"Oh, joy." Her father steered her out of the shop. "Let's get a cup of coffee, shall we?"

Vivian bit back a groan. "Cup of coffee" was code for "let me lecture you" and had been since she was a teenager. Coming on the heels of her mother's comments the day before, she could only imagine what fun the next half hour had in store.

As she walked down the block with her father, she knew she could have made an excuse, could have put him off. But she wanted to know what he had to say, and if the things her mother had told her were true and this seemed the most expedient way to find that out.

After they were settled at a local coffeehouse, her father gave her a very serious look. "You know your mother and I love you and only want what's best for you. Right, Vivian?"

"Of course." Now wasn't the time to argue that. "Why?"

"I think you should pull out of this murder case. It's

not your specialty, not what you're good at. And your name is being ruined. No matter what the outcome is, your reputation is never going to be the same."

"He's innocent, Dad."

"Says you."

"Says the evidence."

"Really? And your vast knowledge in criminal law has shown you this?" He sighed. "Come on, Vivian. If you want to rebel, stick to the battered women's shelters. You don't need to take it this far."

Insult kept her silent for a few seconds as she tried to sort out what she wanted to say first. "Diego's more than a case, Dad. He's a scared kid facing life in prison."

"Which is where he belongs if he killed his pregnant girlfriend. Do you really want to be responsible for letting another animal on the street? I thought you fought against men like this."

"I do—if they're guilty. Diego's not. Besides, it's not like I can get out of this case. It was assigned to me."

"Exactly. You can't tell me Richard actually expected you to win this. If he'd wanted that, he would have put one of the criminal attorneys on it."

"They're already carrying heavy loads. I had an opening." It sounded like an excuse even as she said it.

"Come on, Vivian. You don't believe that." He took his time formulating the rest of his argument, sipping his coffee and watching people at the tables around them. When he finally turned back to her, his face was serious, his blue eyes hard. "You're dragging the family name through the mud with this. We had reporters in the rose garden this morning, trying to get a statement from your mother. It needs to stop."

"I don't know what you expect me to say, Dad. I'm sorry you're being bothered."

"Bothered? You walk around looking like a bum, acting completely out of character, and you say that I'm *bothered?* People are whispering about us at the club, talking about what happened to Merry all those years ago. It's just a matter of time before some reporter digs it up. And then where will we be? Your sister's suicide and the abuse that caused it—will be on the cover of every local paper, as will the fact that her sister is choosing to defend the same kind of man. I won't have it, Vivian. Not the scandal and not you involved with someone publicly accused of that kind of violence."

"So it's the public aspect that has you so bothered, not the violence, right? Because you never seemed bothered by Merry's bruises before."

"That was uncalled for."

"*That* was uncalled for? You're sitting here telling me how to do my job and how to live my life, and you don't even care about me. All you care about is public perception of me, and in turn, you and mother."

She stood up, grabbed her purse. "I'm sorry, Dad, but I can't live my life worried about what other people think."

"Don't kid yourself. The law is nine-tenths perception."

"No, Dad. The law is nine-tenths truth—and that's an entirely different thing."

CHAPTER TEN

As SHE WALKED AWAY from her father, Vivian couldn't help thinking about Rafael and his insistence that he was innocent despite the five years he'd spent in prison. The other night she'd told him she didn't believe him, but she wasn't sure that was true.

Would she really be this attracted to him if she thought he was a rapist? Would she really have let him kiss her and touch her if she thought there was a chance he could turn violent?

No matter what had happened fifteen years before, she couldn't ignore his tenderness with her, the gentle way he held her, the way he never pushed, always made sure that she wanted to be touched before he ever made a move.

The way he'd saved her from being raped by Nacho and his friends.

Those weren't the marks of a rapist or an abuser—she'd dealt with enough in her career to know that much.

But did that mean he'd never been dangerous, or just that he'd turned his life around? She didn't know the answer to those questions, but she wasn't ready to walk away from him yet. The fact of the matter was, she wasn't going on a date with the man he'd been fifteen years ago. She was dating the man he was now, and the man she knew fought for people who needed help. That's why she'd accepted the date with him—because she admired the man he had proven himself to be.

Was that good enough for her? Was she going to be able to build something with him, never knowing for certain if he'd committed such a terrible crime? That was something else she couldn't answer yet, but she knew, for the first time in a very long while, that she wanted to try.

As she climbed into the car, she couldn't help contrasting Rafael's strength with her father's weakness. Doing right by Diego was more important to Rafael than worrying about what had happened to himself all those years before. Her father was worried about the press dragging up Merry's story, and Vivian realized Rafael must have some of the same worries about his own past. The difference was, he hadn't abandoned Diego, hadn't tried to cut himself off from the kid to protect himself.

For no good reason, she was seized by a desire to see Rafael as she pulled into traffic. Before she could talk herself out of it, she flipped a quick U-turn and headed to the center. Surely he wouldn't mind if she just stopped by for a few minutes….

Of course, by the time she'd pulled into the parking lot behind the center she was trying to think of a reasonable excuse as to why she was there. But her mind was blank, and as she climbed out of the car, she had the sick feeling she was going to make a total idiot of herself.

She didn't even look decent, her father had been right

about that much. She was dressed in old jeans and her favorite Harvard Law sweatshirt. The latter had a hole under the right armpit that she'd been ignoring for months, because the shirt was just too comfortable to give up. What was Rafael going to think?

Then again, she mused as she headed for the center, maybe she could use her lack of grooming to her advantage. What woman stalked the man she was interested in while looking like this?

"I thought that was your car I saw pass the basketball courts. Is everything okay?" Rafael met her at the back door, still sweaty from the basketball game he'd been playing, and somehow looking hotter than ever. His T-shirt was plastered to his chest and stomach, showing off enough muscles to make up an eight- or ten-pack— forget the old six-pack her girlfriends liked to drool over.

And his arms—she'd never seen him in short sleeves before and his biceps held her attention for much too long. She tried to yank her gaze away, to come up with something to say like a normal person, but all she could think about was how good it had felt to be hugged by him.

Still, she needed to say something. "Yeah, everything's fine." Now that was an absolutely scintillating conversational starter. Surely she could do better. Trying to look as if it was perfectly natural for her to drop by the center, she asked, "How's Diego?"

Rafael stepped aside to let her in, and as she passed him, she got her first whiff of him. It wasn't fair. How the hell could he smell so good when he'd been sweating? Most guys smelled like stale corn chips and old gym socks after they'd been working out.

Oh no; why should he make it easy on her? He smelled like the ocean—a little salty, a little sweet and completely wild.

"He's doing okay. The doctors say he's young and strong, so he should heal pretty quickly."

Rafael didn't sound pleased, though. Glancing behind her, Vivian did her best to ignore the sexual attraction so she could converse like a normal human being. "You don't sound convinced."

"I'm not." He led her past his office and the rec room and down a hallway she hadn't noticed before. "He's really depressed."

"Well, that's to be expected, isn't it? I mean, he's lost basically his entire family. He's accused of a crime he didn't commit. In my opinion, he's got a lot to be depressed about."

The look Rafael shot her over his shoulder said more than words.

"Oh, you mean suicidally depressed," she murmured. Pictures of her sister flashed into her mind, but she pushed them down. She wouldn't let her feelings for Merry intrude here.

"Yeah," he sighed as he unlocked a door at the end of the hall. "That's exactly what I'm afraid of."

"What is this?" she asked, as she followed him inside the darkened room.

"My apartment." He flipped a switch and suddenly the room was flooded with light. "I need a shower."

"I didn't know you lived on the premises."

He shrugged. "Yeah, well, when I first opened Helping Hands, we were operating on a shoestring budget.

I needed to be here almost all the time, anyway, and living here cut down on my salary."

"And now?"

"Now I'm used to it. I can afford to move out, but why bother? I still spend most of my time here."

She nodded and tried to look as if she understood, when inside she was reeling. How many men did she know who were willing to sacrifice so much of themselves for a cause they believed in, to put the needs of a bunch of underprivileged kids above themselves?

None that she knew of, save Rafael.

An awkward silence stretched between them and finally she said, "Go take your shower. I'll be fine."

"Help yourself to a drink—I think I've got some cold stuff in the fridge."

"Thanks."

"No problem," he said as he headed for what she assumed was his bedroom. Her last glimpse was of his well-defined back as he disappeared inside the room, pulling his T-shirt over his head as he went.

She wandered about the living room as she waited, impressed by how comfortable he'd made the small space. One wall was dominated by a huge navy leather sofa and ottoman. There were a few throw pillows in shades of blue and gray in its corners and what looked like an extra-large, homemade afghan draped across the back. His mother? she wondered, as she fingered the sophisticated pattern. Or an ex-girlfriend with mad crocheting skills? Vivian hoped it was his mother.

Another wall was taken up by what she considered the requisite guy stuff—a decent-size flat-screen TV, a

DVD player and a bunch of stereo equipment. But it was the side wall that really held her interest. It was packed with books of all shapes and sizes, interspersed with some surprisingly sophisticated pieces of pottery. A few snapshots—sans frames—as well as some really beautiful replications of Mayan and Incan art, were scattered about.

As she glanced at the well-worn volumes, she found everything from the philosophical works of Sartre and Camus, to books on the politics and economics of the third world, to biographies of famous artists. Mixed in were quite a few novels that had topped both the literary and mass-market lists. It was an intriguing collection, one that was surprisingly similar to her own. On the top shelf, she spotted a biography she'd been thinking of buying, and wondered what he'd thought of it.

"Did you get something to drink?" Rafael asked as he came through the bedroom door. She tried not to stare at his ripped stomach, and was relieved when he finally covered it with a faded 49ers T-shirt.

Thank God he seemed oblivious to her staring.

"Um, no, not yet. I was just checking out your books."

"See anything you like?

If only he knew. "I've been wanting to read that biography on Frida Kahlo. I love her paintings."

"Yeah, me, too." He reached in the fridge and pulled out a Dr. Pepper and offered it to her. "Take the book with you when you go."

"Are you sure?" Vivian popped the top of the soda and took a sip. "Between Diego's case and my other work, I'm completely bogged down. It may be weeks before I can read it."

He shrugged. "I've already read it, so I'm in no hurry to get it back. Take it if you want it."

She got the feeling he was talking about more than the book. His eyes challenged her. Dared her to step outside her boring world of court cases and long, lonely nights. Tempted her to reach out and take what she wanted for once, without worrying about the consequences.

And she wanted to—God, did she ever. She just didn't know how.

INDECISION WAS WRITTEN all over Vivian's face and he wanted to push her. Wanted to push and push and push until she ended up where she belonged—under him in bed, where he could do to her every wicked, wild thing he'd been imagining.

But he couldn't bring himself to do it. She had to want him enough to come to him.

Well, wasn't he turning out to be the gentleman? Sensitive and sweet and oh so considerate.

And, he told himself, it had nothing at all to do with that Harvard Law sweatshirt she wore so effortlessly, while he'd worked so many hours that he'd barely managed to squeak through at San Francisco State— after he'd been released from prison.

He took a long swallow from his bottle of water and then settled himself on the couch, gesturing for her to do the same. But the second she got close, he realized he'd made a strategic error. She smelled fresh and warm, and his body was responding.

Deciding he needed cooling off in a bad way, he said, "So, I've been talking to more people in Esme's neighborhood, trying to see if the police overlooked someone."

She leaned forward. "What did they say?"

"So far nothing. But a few of them were nervous, too nervous. I didn't push, but I wanted to."

"Give me their names—I'll do it. Things look different with a legal seal attached."

"That's kind of what I was thinking." A strand of hair had fallen into her eye, and he brushed it out of the way. He liked to see her eyes.

She cleared her throat. "Have you talked to anyone else? I'd love to have something concrete before I go into that hearing on Friday."

"I'm going to stop by Esme's place. When Diego and I were talking this morning, he mentioned that he thought one of his attackers sounded like Esme's brother Ricardo.

"The prosecution is going to play it like the beating was payback."

"Maybe it was."

"You don't look convinced."

"I'm not." He took another sip of water, tried to communicate his instincts. "Word is her brothers are in serious trouble—some drugs went missing, and their supplier wants them back."

"And you think he killed Esme instead of going after *them?*"

"If he goes after them, he'll never get his money or the drugs."

"That's disgusting."

"I agree. Which is why I think it's worth paying the

brothers a visit. Could be they're trying to deflect attention off of themselves and onto Diego."

"I'm coming with you."

"I don't think that's a good idea."

"I was stating a fact, not looking for an opinion."

"You wish." There was no way he was taking her into the dirtiest, darkest area of the Tenderloin.

"I *know*." She glanced around. "Do you have a notepad?"

"Sure." He walked to the kitchen and got one out of his junk drawer. "What for?"

"I need to take notes. Who did you see today? What did they say, exactly? And then I want to plan for what we're going to ask when we see Esme's brothers later."

"Vivian! I'm serious—you're not going with me."

The look she leveled at him was just as determined. "I'd like to see you try to stop me."

She turned back to the notebook and began taking notes, when all he wanted to do was pull his hair out at the roots. So much for the docile, little rich girl of his imagination. Vivian had claws, and how sick was it that those claws only made her that much more attractive to him?

THREE HOURS LATER, Vivian was walking through an area of the Tenderloin that made Ellis Street look tame. Drug addicts lined the street, looking for money—or an easy mark—and prostitutes plied their trade on every corner. Homeless people wandered the streets, wine bottles clutched in their dirty fists, and low-riding cars cruised by, filled with boys wearing gang colors and carrying guns.

"Not exactly your typical Christmas scene, huh?"

"Not exactly."

"When we get there, I want you to let me do the talking." Rafael repeated the same instructions he'd given her before they left the community center. "These guys don't respect women and they don't respect authority. It's survival of the fittest out here and the only thing they do respect is the guy who's stronger and faster than they are."

"And that's you."

He ran a teasing eye over her as they turned the corner, stepping past two young prostitutes and a pimp not much older than Diego. "Well, it sure isn't you. You're so scrawny you look like a strong wind could blow you over."

As the cold breeze battered them, Vivian wished she'd thought to grab the jacket she always kept in the trunk of her car. Evenings in San Francisco were always cool, but with Christmas approaching, the temperatures were dipping toward freezing. Not that it looked much like Christmas down here. The bleak, depressing streets made her appreciate the cheery rec room at Helping Hands even more.

"Where does Esme's family live?" she asked, shivering.

"Right here."

Rafael stopped in front of a wooden house that had seen better decades. It had at one time been painted a bright yellow, like so many San Francisco homes. But time and lack of care had worn it down until there was more primer and wood showing than paint.

Junk was piled in the yard and two of the upstairs windows were broken. Someone had taped cardboard over the holes, but it had been there so long that the tape had faded and the cardboard was nearly translucent.

"Esme lived *here?*" Vivian whispered, her heart clenching at the thought of a young, pregnant girl living in such a depressing place. Had she had proper nutrition? Or even hygienic conditions?

It seemed ridiculous to worry about the nutrition of a girl who had died ten weeks earlier, but Vivian couldn't help glancing up and down the street and asking herself how many other girls were living in the same squalid situation.

"Remember—"

"I know, I know." She gingerly climbed the rotting steps. "I'll let you do all the talking."

He looked doubtful as he knocked on the door. "I'm serious, Vivian."

"I know you are. It's—" She stopped midsentence when it swung open.

A woman stood there. No more than five feet tall, even with her hair pulled into a severe bun at the top of her hair. She looked tired. And defeated. As if life had finally got the best of her and she'd given up fighting the bad parts.

"*Hola,* Rafael." Her hands twisted in the faded skirt of her housedress and her sad eyes grew even sadder as she looked at him. "*Cómo estés?*"

"*Bien,* Marta. *Y tú?*"

The two spoke in Spanish for a couple minutes, and Vivian remembered just enough from college to understand that Esme's brothers were sleeping, but that Marta was going to wake them up—at Rafael's insistence.

She ushered them into a family room with a faded, broken-down couch and a three-thousand-dollar, flat-screen TV. The dichotomy amazed Vivian. Who would choose to spend that much on a television set, but not on the house in which they lived?

A few minutes passed in silence as she and Rafael stood staring at a cooking show blaring in Spanish. Rafael gestured for her to sit down, but she was too scared of the numerous, suspicious stains on the couch to do more than stand near it and pretend absorption in the television program.

Finally, just when she'd decided that Esme's brothers weren't going to show up, they ambled down the stairs. Both were dressed in oversize jerseys and baggy jeans, and both looked mean as hell.

Her first glimpse of them had any thought of taking notes at this meeting skittering away once and for all. No wonder Rafael had shot her a look of pitying amusement on their way here.

A quick glance at Rafael had her starting in surprise. Gone was the understanding when he'd stared at Marta, and in its place was a glare so fierce she could only be grateful it wasn't aimed at her.

The two men on the stairs didn't seem overly intimidated, though the second one did shift uneasily under the scrutiny, his right hand going to the waistband of his jeans.

"Rafael—" She started to warn him that something wasn't right, but he simply put a calming hand on her shoulder before stepping slightly in front of her as if to shield her.

But she didn't want him to—she wanted to get as far away from this place as she could. There had to be another way to get the information they needed to help Diego.

Rafael was calm though, and she told herself to settle down. After all, she was the one who'd insisted on coming on this quick little jaunt into hell.

"Rafael, what are you doing here, man?"

"Hey, Danny. Ric." He nodded at them with a half smile, not showing by word or deed that he was in any way uncomfortable. Vivian tried to follow his lead, and put on her best poker face, but she had a feeling she looked more sick than relaxed. She couldn't get her lips to do more than curve in a parody of a smile.

"Get out. And take your little whore for hire with you."

Vivian felt Rafael tense, but he kept his voice smooth and easy when he said, "Is that how your mother raised you to talk to women?"

"It's how she raised me to talk to bitch lawyers who are defending the asshole who killed my little sister."

"We all know Diego didn't kill Esme, Danny. So why don't you save the posturing?"

"That's bull, man," said the one who looked like a serial killer. "He did her. He got her pregnant, and then killed her when she and the baby got to be too much trouble."

"You really believe that?"

"Damn straight."

"Then why's he still alive?"

Danny got right in his face. "Because I want that little prick to spend the rest of his life in a cage. A member of the living dead." He paused, then pulled the gun. "But I don't have the same wish for you, so why don't you take your skinny, little, skanky lawyer and get the hell out of my mama's house. She doesn't want you here."

"That's a lot of cursing and protesting for two guys who claim Diego's the bad guy."

The gun never wavered. "What do you mean by that?"

"You know exactly what I mean. Maybe your…extracurricular activities came back to bite you in the ass and Esme was just collateral damage."

"You don't know what you're talking about!"

"Don't I?" Rafael towered over him, using every inch of his height to intimidate Danny.

"You think we'd let some coked-out *pendejo* kill her? Esme was our sister!"

Rafael shook his head with a snarl. "Don't act like you give a shit about that. You never liked her. I've heard you going on about her any number of times, talking about how she was too stuck-up for her own good."

"That doesn't mean we wanted her dead." Ric spoke up for the first time, his voice filled with a desperation that raised Vivian's eyebrows—and her suspicions.

"No. But it also doesn't mean that you'd throw yourself in front of traffic for her, either. Which makes your preoccupation with Diego more than a little suspect."

"He raped and murdered our baby sister!"

"Did he, Ric? Or is he just an easy fall guy while the guy who really did her gets away with murder?" Rafael's smile was a deadly threat. "What's a little murder between friends, anyway?"

Danny leveled his gun straight at Rafael's head.

Biting back the scream that rose instinctively in her throat, Vivian reached for Rafael. He shook her off, while he made sure his body was between hers and the gun.

"You're about to find out. You have exactly twenty seconds to get out of my house, or I'm going to blow your brains out."

"I'm going to find out what happened to Esme, Danny."

"You know what happened to her—her punk-ass boyfriend killed her. And you're protecting him."

"No." Rafael stared the kid down, and Vivian watched in alarm as the gun began to shake. "Someone else killed your sister. Someone who's finding it really easy to hide behind Diego. That stops now."

"He killed her." Ric's voice was desperate, his eyes wild as he moved forward to stand next to his brother. "*Diego* killed her. Everyone knows that."

"I don't know it, and neither does his attorney. We're going to find out what happened. If you know, if you were involved, it's better to come clean now before all hell breaks loose."

"You're sick, man. We never would have hurt our sister."

Rafael stared at him until he was forced to drop his eyes. "Can the same be said for all of your associates?"

"Get outta my house!" Danny's voice was louder than before, more anxious. There must have been something in it that triggered Rafael's radar because suddenly he was moving as if the house were on fire, grabbing Vivian's arm and shoving her toward the front door.

"We're leaving. But we're not going to let this go, Danny. *I'm* not going to let it go."

"Screw you, man. Your little boy's gonna fry."

"If he does, I'll make sure he's not the only one. Remember that."

As Rafael closed the door behind them, Vivian half expected to hear a gun go off, was scared to death that she was going to look up and see Rafael covered in blood, but to her surprise—and undying gratitude—nothing happened.

They didn't speak until they'd gotten up the block and around the corner.

Finally, when she was sure Danny and Ric weren't lurking somewhere, prepared to gun them down, she hissed at Rafael, "Have you lost your mind? You all but issued them an ultimatum."

"Diego's in the hospital, you're being threatened—you're damn right I issued them an ultimatum. And if things go as planned, they'll come after me to make sure I don't deliver."

"Is that was this is about? Setting yourself up as bait? Are you kidding me? That's your big plan—sacrificing yourself for Diego?"

The look he gave her was inscrutable. "I'm not planning on sacrificing anything, but I am going to shake the trees until I find the bastards that did this to Esme. With any luck, I'll make enough noise that they'll come after me. Then I'm going to burn them all."

"How do you know her brothers know anything about that? Wouldn't they come forward to get justice for their sister?"

"Give me a break, Vivian. They're running scared and we both know it. You narrowed in on these guys from the first time you spoke with Diego, and nothing besides that gun has happened to change your mind.

"Those boys are scared spitless. And not just of me—they were too strung-out, too adamant. Guys don't roll like that down here unless something big's at risk.

"Those two know a lot more about what happened than they're saying, and I'm not going to see Diego spend the rest of his life in jail just because those morons got themselves in too deep with someone a lot badder than they are."

"Still, what if something happens to you?"

He looked at her sideways. "Would you miss me?"

"Not at all. I just don't want to be standing near you when the bullet hits. Blood can be so hard to get out of good silk."

"You're hilarious."

"Don't ask stupid questions if you don't want stupid answers."

He laughed and the tension dissipated from his face as if it had never been. "You're pretty fabulous, you know that?"

"I *have* heard that before." She smiled up at him.

"Then it's obviously a sentiment that bears repeating." Reaching out, he grabbed her hand and twined their fingers together.

The fact that she let him told her everything she needed to know about her feelings toward Rafael—even as it scared the hell out of her.

CHAPTER ELEVEN

WHAT HAD HE BEEN THINKING? Rafael wondered early the next evening as he helped Vivian into his truck. What had possessed him to think it would be a good idea to take her out? Even worse, to bring her to meet his family?

He circled around to his side of the vehicle and climbed in. He tried to smile at her as he started the ignition, but from the expression on her face, his smile had come across even more sickly than he'd been afraid of.

He'd woken up that morning with an ill feeling in the pit of his stomach, and his first glimpse of her apartment had only made things worse. He'd known from the beginning that she had money, but that didn't quite cover it. She was filthy rich.

Ivory tower rich.

So rich that her pocket change could probably buy him three times over.

And he was bringing her to his parents' restaurant to meet his family—on their first date. Was he completely insane? What if she didn't like his family, or God forbid, pitied them?

What if she reminded them of the last woman he'd brought home who was out of her element? Normally his family did its best to pretend those five years hadn't happened. Was bringing Vivian to the party waving a red flag?

"Rafael?" Vivian asked quietly. "Is everything okay? With Diego, I mean?"

"I think so. I haven't talked to him since this afternoon, but he sounded as good as could be expected then. Why?"

"You seem…different."

"I'm sorry. It's just been a long couple of days." Forcing a smile, he glanced at her, doing his best to keep his eyes off the large, perfectly wrapped box on her lap. It screamed expensive and was just one more thing that was making the collar of his dress shirt feel too tight.

"I know that feeling." The smile she sent him was a lot warmer than he deserved. "I've been working like crazy to try to get as much evidence lined up as I can for the hearing tomorrow. I contacted someone I know in Vice, who was able to back up Ric's and Danny's involvement in dealing, and the school finally came through with Diego's records. They're completely clean."

Rafael eased off the freeway and took the first left, told himself to concentrate on what he could control. "Do you need me to testify?" he asked, a cold drop of sweat rolling down his back as he checked the clock.

They were only a couple of miles from his mom and dad's place now, and everyone should already be there. Part of him wanted to delay the inevitable, and the other half wanted to just get it over with.

"Not yet. This is early days." She tossed her hair behind her shoulder and he barely kept himself from groaning. Why had she chosen tonight of all nights to leave her hair down? He was supposed to be paying attention to the road, but he kept imagining what it would feel like to wrap himself up in all that hair as he kissed every inch of her.

He tried to focus on something else, told himself he wouldn't try to rush her into bed. It was enough that she'd agreed to go out with him knowing his past. Asking for more would be a blueprint for disaster.

Though he knew he was doing the right thing, the dress Vivian was wearing was driving him nuts. Even with her coat on, it exposed luscious glimpses of her breasts and legs.

"When would you need me to testify?" He said it with the desperation of a man grasping his last lifeline, but surely focusing on Diego's plight would help keep his mind off his own.

She shrugged. "It depends on what happens from this point on."

Rafael shot her a quick look. "Meaning?"

"Meaning that as soon as I get the judge to agree to hear the case in juvenile court, I'll be filing for a dismissal, based on the lack of state's evidence. If that fails, I'll go after the little bit of evidence they do have."

"And if that doesn't work?"

"Then a trial date will be set, and when it comes up, I'll need you to testify to Diego's character." She reached over and placed a hand on his knee as if to comfort him. "Of course, by the time that comes to pass, we should have found at least one witness who saw someone other than Diego near Esme's house. Plus, by then, the private detective I hired might actually have something concrete on Barnes and Turner."

"The report didn't turn up anything."

"It turned up a whole lot of suspicions, but nothing substantial. Seems to be the story of my life right now, and it's driving me nuts. They've been in disciplinary hearings twice, but never suspended. There are credible rumors that they're dirty, but…"

"The boys in blue protect their own."

"Exactly."

He reached beneath the damn present and squeezed her hand. "I don't think I've said thank-you for everything you're doing for Diego."

She smiled. "You're welcome."

"You're doing a hell of a job." And she was. She'd turned over stones he hadn't thought to mess with, like with the cops. Sure, he'd thought they were prejudiced against Diego, but he'd never thought to dig deeper, to see if they had another motive for their incompetence.

Vivian had. She was thorough and tough and more than willing to play every card she had to get a winner. The differences between her and the public defender Diego first had were so huge that it was hard to imagine they were both in the same profession.

Rafael stopped at a red light and turned to gaze at her. She looked beautiful in the dim light of the street-lamps, her peaches-and-cream profile perfect against the darkness.

Ignoring his erection, he carried the hand he still held to his mouth and pressed a soft kiss on her open palm.

Her pulse jumped under his fingers and her eyes

widened. In confusion? he wondered. Or desire? He didn't know, and for the moment he was content not to analyze.

She felt so good beside him, her soft body only inches from his own. The cab of his truck filled with her sweet scent, which wrapped itself around him, made him want her more than he could ever remember wanting another woman.

"I'm only doing for Diego what any decent lawyer would."

"That's not true." He ran his thumb over the back of her hand. "You're doing so much more than I ever expected."

The light turned green, but he didn't let go of her hand. Reveled in the fact that she made no move to let go of his.

She didn't say anything else until they were pulling into a parking spot at the back of his parents' restaurant, and then she whispered, "I don't want your gratitude."

His heart jumped as he wondered what she did want from him. For a moment he could think of nothing but leaping on top of her. It had been a long time since he'd taken a woman in his truck, but—

He stopped himself before he got any further. Hadn't he just promised himself he wouldn't push her? That he'd be content with what she wanted to give him? Too bad his libido hadn't caught up with his conscience.

Holding himself steady, Rafael turned off the engine and then did the most stupid thing imaginable. He asked softly, "What *do* you want?"

Vivian's hand tensed in his and she glanced away. The silence between them stretched so long that he was sure she wouldn't answer him. But just as disappointment filled him, just as he told himself it was better this way, she whispered, "You."

He groaned, and reached for her as all his good intentions went out the window. Pulling her across the seat, he scooted to the middle, then settled her in his lap.

Her fingers gripped his shoulders, while his hands tangled in her hair. He wanted to get closer to her, wanted to be inside her—not just her body but her beautiful, beautiful soul.

He lowered his mouth to hers and had one glorious moment to savor the taste of her—the unbelievable, addictive taste of her—before someone pounded on the hood of his truck. Laughter exploded around them and then Gabriel's voice sounded right outside the driver's window.

"Come on, Rafa. Do the lovebird routine later! You're late. Miguel and Heather should be showing up any second now. Mama wants you inside so you can hide with the rest of us."

Vivian was squirming away from him before Gabriel had finished his first sentence, her face flaming red in the dim lights of the parking lot. "It's okay," Rafael said, trying to soothe her, to pull her back against him. But she was having none of it.

She bent and picked up the present she'd brought for Miguel, then hid behind the large box. "Don't be embarrassed," he said softly, watching her. "There's no reason to be."

"Are you kidding me? How can I be anything but embarrassed?" she hissed. "I almost had sex with you in the parking lot of your parents' restaurant! In your truck! In front of people I can only assume are your friends and relatives!"

He nearly crowed at the acknowledgment that she was as willing—and obviously anxious—to make love to him as he was to her. Part of him wanted nothing more than to tell Gabriel to buzz off so he could pull her into his lap again and show her exactly how good it could be in a parked vehicle.

How good it *would* be between them, anywhere.

"It's just my brother Gabriel and a couple of his friends. He's the second oldest, so he takes his responsibility to harass and humiliate us seriously."

"I can see that," she murmured. "Please let him know that he's succeeded—at least on my part."

"Don't worry about him," Rafael repeated, before sliding from the car with a muttered warning to his brother to lay off. Then he walked around the truck to help Vivian out. She kept her face turned away as she slid from the passenger's seat, and refused to look at Rafael even after he'd called her name.

He wasn't willing to budge on this and before she could slip by him, he caught her chin between his thumb and index finger and pressed just hard enough to force her to meet his eyes. "Don't be embarrassed," he said. "Gabriel's happily married to a beautiful woman, and believe me, I've caught them doing much worse more times than I can count."

"Stop it!" she whispered fiercely, trying to pull away. "You're not going to make me feel better."

"But it's true." Gabriel said with a wink as he

extended his hand to shake hers. "And hey, it's about time Rafael found a nice woman to hang around with. Mom worries about him, since he's such a loner. Like a bear with a sore paw."

Rafael watched his brother's interaction with Vivian tensely, waiting for some clue as to what he was thinking. But if he was upset Rafa had brought an obviously wealthy, obviously fancy woman to the party, he certainly didn't show it.

Did that mean he was hiding his concerns, or that Rafael had blown the whole thing out of proportion? As attached as he was growing to Vivian, he could only hope it was the latter.

VIVIAN HAD NEVER BEEN more embarrassed in her life, but she figured at this point it was better to brazen things out than to curl up in the fetal position and try to disappear. "It's nice to meet you, Gabriel," she murmured as she clasped his hand, which was almost as big and nearly as rough as Rafael's, in her own.

But his smile was more open, more relaxed, and she couldn't help responding to him. "Rafael didn't tell me this was a surprise party."

"Yeah, well, Rafael doesn't say much more than he has to, or haven't you figured that out already?" Gabriel draped an arm around her shoulder and guided her toward the restaurant.

"I'm beginning to realize that," she said, glancing at Rafael from beneath her lashes. "But I'd love to hear any other tips you've got for me?"

Gabriel threw back his head and laughed, then opened

the door of the restaurant and shouted, "Mama, Dad. Come see what Rafael brought. You'll love her."

"Well, bring her in then, *mijo.*"

As she walked into the restaurant, Vivian was greeted by a tall, curvy woman whose beauty was as fierce as her son's.

"Hi, Mama." Rafael leaned down and kissed his mother's cheek. She hugged him tightly before returning the kiss.

"Now introduce me to your beautiful friend, Rafael." Her eyes were bright and inquisitive as she turned to Vivian.

"This is Vivian Wentworth. Vivian, this is my mother, Angelina."

"Hello, Mrs. Cardoza." Vivian glanced around at the brightly decorated room. "Your restaurant is lovely."

"Thank you. It's hard work, but we love it. And please, call me Angelina." She took the present from Vivian's hands and handed it to Gabriel. "Go put this on the table with the others. And hurry—your brother will be here soon.

"And you…" She looked at Rafael. "You go get Vivian a drink. There's fresh margaritas and sangria at the bar. What would you like, *niña?*"

"A margarita sounds great."

"Got it, and for you, Mama?" Vivian watched, amused, as Rafael hopped to do his mother's bidding.

"Make it two."

As soon as he walked away, Angelina looped her arm through Vivian's and pulled her deeper into the room. "So, tell me about yourself, Vivian. What do you do?"

"I'm an attorney."

"Oh, yes. That's why you look familiar—you're defending one of Rafa's kids on that horrible murder charge. I've seen you on TV."

Vivian didn't know quite how to respond to that—the media hadn't exactly been showing her best side.

"The press—they're vultures. When Rafael was in trouble years ago, they used to hound us mercilessly," Angelina said. She shook her head as if to clear it. "Anyway. You're a lawyer and you're a native of San Francisco?"

"I am. My parents are from Boston, but they moved here before I was born."

"Boston's a nice city—too cold for me. I was born in Rio."

"Now that's a beautiful city!"

"It is, yes. But crazy. I took the boys to Carnaval when they were teenagers." She rolled her eyes. "They got into so much trouble, but had such a good time I couldn't yell at them. And Rafa, he was the worst. That boy was always getting into something." Angelina laughed softly.

"That doesn't surprise me—he looks like trouble."

"Oh, you have no idea." She pointed to her head. "Half my gray hairs come from him."

Vivian looked at her hostess's sleek black hair. "I don't see any gray."

"That's because I have a good hairdresser, but that doesn't mean they aren't there."

It was Vivian's turn to laugh.

"Now, tell me more."

Those words started the madness, and for the next four hours, Vivian was passed from one member of Rafael's family to another.

Roberto Cardoza was a charming man, who plied her with margaritas and with stories of his youngest son while he danced her around and around the small wooden floor at the center of the restaurant. He laughed and flirted outrageously, and as she smiled into his still-handsome face, she got a glimpse of what Rafael would look like in another thirty-five years or so. It was a nice image.

Each of his brothers also claimed her for a dance, including the birthday boy, Miguel, who was as serious as Gabriel was jovial.

No wonder Rafael had turned out so well, she told herself, as she whirled and spun, laughed and joked with Rafael's family.

No wonder he was so compassionate and caring toward all those kids. His parents had given him such unconditional love….

"Having fun?" Rafa asked the first time he managed to catch up to her. He held out a glass of water, which she gulped down thirstily.

"Your father's a wild man."

"Only with the people he likes."

"Well, he must love me then," she teased. "I can't remember the last time I danced so much."

"I think he's crazy about you."

"Well, the feeling's entirely mutual. Your family is fabulous, and you're so different when they're around."

"What do you mean?" His eyes searched hers warily.

"I mean, you smiled more in the first hour you were

here than you have in the entire time I've known you. You're happy here."

"Of course—this is home. Isn't that what family is for?"

"It's supposed to be."

Vivian thought of her own family, of the layers and layers of ice between them and any real emotions. She couldn't remember the last time she'd had a conversation with her mother that didn't include full emotional body armor. And yet here, everything was so effortless, so joyous. Rafael's mother was so far away from Lillian Wentworth in style and attitude that she might as well have been a different species.

Vivian wanted to talk to him more, to spend some time analyzing this Rafael. Here his defenses were down, he was relaxed, calm, centered in a way she never saw when he was fighting for Diego. It was a whole new side of him, one she found exponentially attractive.

But just as she was leaning in to kiss him, his youngest sister, Michaela, swooped in and spirited her away. "Hey, no fair hogging Vivian," she called over her shoulder as she pulled her along in her wake. "You get her all the time."

"Make sure you bring her back in one piece, brat!"

"Yeah, yeah, yeah."

They swept into the kitchen. "Some of the trays are empty—you can help me refill them."

"Sure." Vivian glanced around the kitchen cluelessly. "Where do I start?"

"See the big baskets over there? Fill them with chips."

"Okay."

They worked in silence for a couple minutes, then Michaela said, "I love that dress, it's totally cool."

Vivian glanced down at the dress her mother had gotten her for her birthday. "Thanks. I don't wear it very much."

"If I had something couture, I'd wear it every day."

"How do you know it's couture?"

"I'm going to the Art Institute, majoring in fashion design." She grinned as she loaded a tray with fresh sopaipillas. "Fashion is my *life.*"

"I can see that—your scarf is fabulous."

"I made it."

"No way." Vivian stepped closer, ran the fine silk through her hands. "It's gorgeous."

"I know, right? Rafael bought me the material a few months ago, told me he knew I could do something fabulous with it."

"Rafael?"

"Yeah, he's always doing stuff like that, you know? Material for me, a new kitchen tool for Mama. He's a great guy."

Vivian glanced at her, amused. "Is this the part where you tell me all about Rafael's virtues?"

"No," Michaela snapped. "It's the part where I tell you I'll break one of your bones if you hurt him."

"Well. All right." Vivian backed off, started arranging watermelon on a plate. Then, because she couldn't resist, added, "Can I ask which one?"

"Whichever one hurts the most. Look, no offense. You seem really nice, but Rafa's been through the wringer and he can't take much more disappointment."

"I think you're confused about Rafa's and my relationship. This is our first date."

"I don't care if it's your fifty-first. He wouldn't have brought you here if you didn't matter to him, and that's cool. I want him to be happy, believe me. He deserves it. I remember what it was like before, when he wasn't happy. When he wasn't here." She paused. "I much prefer happy."

"I'm not planning on hurting him."

"Good, then don't. He's already had more than his fair share of pain. He doesn't need one more, especially now. This whole thing with Diego's killing him."

"I know."

Michaela's gaze shot to hers. "Do you?"

"Yes." Vivian fought to keep her voice steady. "He told me about his past."

"Wow. He never talks about it. Never." She reached for a sopaipilla and a bottle of honey, then settled on one of the high stools next to the counter. "I was six when it happened, and I didn't understand. How could Rafael be here one day and gone the next? Mama and *Papi*, they would visit him, but I was never allowed to go. It was too dangerous, they would say. No place for a little girl. But I missed my brother, missed the young man who would toss me in the air and laugh when he caught me.

"Miguel and Gabriel aren't like Rafa. They don't always take the time to do the little stuff, but it's the little stuff that makes the difference, you know?" She drenched the sopaipilla in honey, then gave half to Vivian.

"I do know."

"When he came in here today, he was nervous. I mean, really worried about introducing you to us."

Her heart beat a little faster. "How could you tell?"

"He always sticks his left hand in his pocket. And he does that thing with his face." She did a credible imitation of Rafa's downturned mouth and furrowed brow. "Like he's contemplating world peace—or domination."

"I've seen that look before. Are you sure it means he's nervous?"

"I'm positive. He's been doing it his whole life." Michaela stuffed the last of the dessert in her mouth, then hopped off the stool. "We need to get back before Mama comes in here and starts yelling." She grabbed two heavy trays and started out.

Vivian followed her, then spent the rest of the party being passed between aunts, uncles, cousins and family friends as they filled the colorful restaurant to the breaking point. Everyone seemed to want to meet her.

When she was sure she couldn't dance to one more song without a break, she cried "uncle" and made a quick trip to the restroom.

As she splashed water on her overheated cheeks—her makeup had worn off five or six dances before, so she had nothing to worry about on that front—she couldn't help glancing in the mirror. And was surprised by how happy she looked. How at peace, despite Michaela's warnings echoing in her head. Despite her own warnings.

But how could she have known as she dressed for this party that she was going to end up having such a fabulous time? It was nothing like the get-togethers her parents and work colleagues threw. Those were catered and organized with a precision the military could only hope to emulate. And everything was sedate—from the dresses, to the music, to the dancing and conversation. The goal was to see and be seen, and fun rarely factored into it.

She hadn't known what she'd been missing. Oh, she'd hated the parties her parents forced her to attend, and did her best to squeeze out of them when she had the chance. But she'd thought the flaw lay with her—that what had happened to Merry had simply made Vivian herself too uptight, too untrusting, to have a good time.

Tonight had proved it wasn't her, though, she thought in triumph as she applied a fresh coat of the nude lip gloss she wore in the hopes of downplaying her annoyingly crooked mouth. Because she didn't feel dull around these people, didn't feel uncomfortable or annoyed or like she had to escape.

Instead, she felt free. Free of all the social conventions her mother worshipped. Free of all the undercurrents it took so much work to keep up with. Free to be herself, and everything that entailed, good or bad.

Tucking the gloss into her purse, she all but floated to the bathroom door. Maybe she'd be able to snag Rafael for another dance. She had loved the feel of his arms around her earlier, when he'd whirled her about the dance floor to a wild flamenco tune. And she wouldn't mind another margarita, though she'd already had three. She was thirsty, and never before had a citrusy drink tasted so good.

Opening the door with a grin, determined to find Rafael in the crush, she was thrilled when she almost ran facefirst into his broad chest.

"Hey there," he said, with the slow, lazy grin she'd seen so much of tonight. "Where's the fire?" he asked, bending down so that his warm breath brushed against her ear.

"I want to dance with you again. You're really good at it."

"So are you."

She grinned in turn. "Eight years of dance lessons. When I was a child I was totally clumsy, always running into things. Mom enrolled me in ballet and ballroom dancing so I could learn to be more graceful."

They bobbed and weaved their way through the throngs of people, and when they finally reached the dance floor he pulled her into his arms. A slow song was playing—one of the first of the night—and she melted into Rafael. Reveled in the feel of his long, hard body against hers. Relished the fact that she didn't tower above him in her high heels, that she could comfortably rest her head on his shoulder and absorb the incredible masculine scent of him.

He smelled like the ocean, wicked and wild and so incredibly sexy that she wanted to lick him. To taste him.

She must have made a sound that tipped him off, because the muscles of his back and neck grew tense beneath her arms even as his thighs tightened so quickly it had to be painful.

It was a delicious feeling having this incredible man so attuned to her moods that he knew what she wanted before she asked for it. But she didn't move despite his obvious arousal, afraid that if she did, the rosy glow of contentment that she was using to look at the world would shatter around her.

"Do you want to go home?" He whispered the words in her ear as if he, too, was afraid of breaking the moment.

She knew what he was asking, knew that if she left with him now, she'd end up making love with him tonight. She turned the decision over in her head, realized that for once she felt no trepidation, only a sense of rightness she didn't want to deny.

Pulling away from Rafael, she looked him straight in the eye and said, "Come home with me."

CHAPTER TWELVE

THEY DROVE BACK TO HER apartment in silence, the echo of her last words on the dance floor all around them. Her hand was in Rafael's, her thigh pressed against his.

Each bump of the road pressed her more firmly against him, had her excitement ratcheting up another notch until being with him was all she could think about.

She was taking a huge step, putting a lot of trust in him, but after tonight she couldn't do anything else. He'd let her see him with his family, let her see his vulnerabilities, when he prided himself on being strong.

How could she do any less?

By the time they got to her apartment, her blood was pounding through her veins and hunger—raw, out of control, insatiable—was whipping through her. She had no idea what the future, or even the next few days, would bring, but she was determined to have this time with him.

The slam of the door behind them sounded like a gunshot, and it galvanized Rafael to action. With a groan, he lowered his head and captured her mouth with his own.

The moment his warm lips touched hers, her tenuous grip on control vanished. Her hands tangled in the cool silk of his hair as his tongue gently parted her lips. But she didn't want gentleness now, didn't want him to hold back anything out of concern for her. She wanted Rafael, with his black moods and violent quests, with his analytical mind and furious passions. And she would have him. Tonight. Now. This instant.

"Rafael." She whispered his name, clung to him. He was her sanity in a world turned suddenly upside down, the only thing standing between her and her bland, boring past. But she wouldn't think of her reticence now—refused to think of it. Not when Rafael was in her arms and as hungry and needy for her as she was for him.

He kissed her again and it was hot. Electric. All-consuming and terribly addicting.

Self-preservation reared its ugly head, warned her to stop this before it was too late, before she lost everything. But it had been too late the moment he'd first rescued her. Too late from the second he'd kissed her palm and dragged her across his truck and into his lap. Now all she could do was ride the wave and let the collateral damage take care of itself.

Trembling with the pain and pleasure of her desire for him, Vivian parted her lips and let him in.

And he took her. Again and again and again he used his tongue and teeth and lips on her, in her. Sucked her lower lip between his teeth and bit. Ran his tongue soothingly over the little hurt before thrusting it inside of her again.

She moaned low in her throat as their tongues met, dueled, then surrendered. Desire was a burning pain in every part of her, sweeping from her mouth to her breasts to her very core.

"Rafael," she gasped against his lips, her body straining against his.

He laughed then pushed against her with his chest, his legs, his iron-hard thighs. She whimpered, liquid heat rushing through the very heart of her until the only thing keeping her upright was him.

Still he pushed, backing her across the room. Lifting her. Pressing against her until she was trapped between the wall and his rigid body. He settled between her legs, his hardness cradled by her sex, and she moaned in helpless pleasure.

"Take me." She arched against him, her body an open invitation as she circled his waist with her legs. "Take me now."

He laughed again, then thrust himself against her.

She nearly came despite the layers of clothes separating them from the ultimate union.

"There's no reason to rush, sweetheart. We've got all night." He ran his tongue down her throat, following a bead of sweat as it ran into the valley between her breasts. "I want to savor you."

"There's every reason to rush," she answered, clawing at the fine silk of his shirt with her fingers. The material tore beneath her attack and then there was nothing stopping her from exploring the broad expanse of chiseled muscles. "I'm going to die if you don't come inside me. Now." She dug her nails into his skin and relished his instantaneous response.

In that moment, Rafael lost the control he'd been so valiantly struggling to hold on to. Before he could think better of it, before he could even attempt to calm himself down, he tangled his hands in her hair. Her head hit the wall hard, but neither of them noticed as he ground his mouth to hers and plundered.

She tasted bittersweet, like pain and pleasure and every craving he'd ever had. Breaking away from her lips, he ran his tongue down her throat. Tore at her clothes with his hands and teeth until her dress slipped to the floor.

He was desperate, completely enthralled by the heat pouring off her in waves. He had to taste her, touch her, push himself inside of her until—

"Rafael!" He kissed his way down her breasts, then pulled back a little so that he could see her gorgeous nipples. They were the sweetest shade of pink he'd ever seen—the same color as her glorious, topsy-turvy mouth.

Closing his teeth over one sweet bud, he bit her softly and nearly imploded with his first taste. Her screams of pleasure echoed in his ears.

He switched to the other nipple, drew it into his mouth and rolled it between his teeth. Vivian was crying, moaning, her soft, seductive body bucking against him with each pull of his mouth on her breast.

"Now, now, now." she repeated the word like a litany, her back bowed. He raised his head and looked at her, then stood transfixed for a moment by her incredible beauty.

She was too far gone to appreciate his restraint, and he felt his last hold on sanity abandon him as she moved against him. "Rafael, please! Please," she chanted, sobs racking her chest until her entire body shuddered against him.

And still he continued, taking her further than she'd

ever gone before. Taking her outside of herself and into him until she ceased to exist as an entity separate from him. There was no more Vivian, no more court case, no more danger. There was only Rafael and the incredible, terrifying control he exerted over every part of her.

Rafael laughed as he slid a finger inside of her and found her most sensitive spot. He rubbed against her— once, twice—and just that easily hurtled her into the most intense orgasm of her life.

As she stood there, afraid to move because she knew her shaky legs wouldn't support her, he pulled her against his chest with one fluid movement, then carried her through her apartment.

"Where's your bedroom?" he murmured, his voice so low that it might have been a growl. His eyes glowed like obsidian in the dim hallway light.

"To the right." It was all she could do to get the words out, her body thrumming with need despite the release she had just had. Her feelings for him had welled up inside of her until the ache was as much emotional as physical.

She needed him. Craved him. Was dying to feel him inside of her. She tried to tell him so, but the connections between her brain and the rest of her body seemed to have short-circuited, and all she could do was moan. So she simply relaxed as he found her bedroom and laid her on the lavender satin comforter she'd bought a few months before.

He pulled away and she whimpered, tried to reach for him, but he merely laughed, and she could hear the rustle of clothes in the darkness. Determined to see him, she rolled to her side and extended a lazy, languorous hand toward the base of the lamp on her dresser. A dim light appeared, one that was soft and rosy and oh so inviting.

Then she settled back on the bed and enjoyed the show as Rafael unbuttoned his pants and slowly stripped them off his long, heavily muscled thighs.

He was beautiful, so strong, so tender he made her ache. Captivated by him, desperate to feel his hardness between her hands, she managed to get her brain to issue one more intelligible order to the rest of her body. Reaching for him, she murmured, "My turn."

He grinned, then settled himself next to her on her big soft bed. "Eventually."

"I don't want to wait that long." She sighed and began to stroke.

The breath slammed out of him as every muscle in Rafael's body tightened to the point of pain. He fought to relax, but that was impossible as her hands and mouth skimmed over his shoulders and chest and stomach. As she moved lower, sparks exploded behind his eyes— clean and bright and almost as beautiful as Vivian's eyes.

"Vivian." Her name was all he could manage to say, a guttural groan, when what he really wanted to do was praise her. To tell her how beautiful she was. How much he wanted and needed her. How he'd do anything for her.

But she was killing him softly, slowly and without a shred of mercy as her mouth skimmed over his thighs.

She was as pale as the ocean in the moonlight, as wild as the waves breaking against the sand, and he couldn't get enough of her. Her long, silky, glorious hair was wrapped around her, wrapped around him, as he brought his hands to her slender, breakable body. It was hard to imagine such strength existed in something so fragile.

"Tell me you want me," he whispered as he pulled her back up his body. He licked his way over every inch of her—down her breasts to the nipples, over the flat plane of her stomach, down the silky sweetness of her thighs to her calves and back up again.

She moaned yet again. "I want you," she breathed, her entire body taught with desire. "I need you. Rafael, oh God, I need you so much."

"I'm here," he answered, lifting his face to look her in her eyes.

"Please," she said, and barely recognized herself. When had she ever begged for anything? Never. But he had a power over her that couldn't be denied.

He snagged his wallet out of the back pocket of his jeans and grabbed a condom. Quickly rolling it over himself, he reached between them and flicked a finger over her once, twice.

Her fingers clutched at his shoulders, her body wildly arching against his. He plunged into her, moving hard and fast against her, intensifying her release, building toward his own.

Leaning down, he drew her nipple into his mouth. Sucked hard as he continued moving inside of her. He was close, so close he thought he'd explode any second. But he wanted to make this last, needed to be inside her forever.

She was sobbing, her hands tangled in his as her body shuddered. "Please, please."

"That's it, baby. Let me feel you." His words were strangled as he moved faster and faster, loving the warm, wet feel of her muscles clenching around him. He lowered his mouth to her breast again, sucked hard even as he reached between them and stroked her.

Vivian cried out, her body bucking against him as another release—more intense and out of control than the first—ripped through her. He rode her through it, took her higher until nothing existed but the rolling pleasure that went on and on. Grabbing her hips, he tilted them until she was open fully to him.

He was going to lose it, couldn't hold back any longer, had to— With a groan he came. The world went dim and he was lost totally to the insane pleasure over-loading his senses. Immersed in the waves of sensation sweeping through him. he was dimly conscious of Vivian's body convulsing again, milking him as he emptied himself inside of her.

When it was over he collapsed on top of her, breathing in harsh, ragged gasps. He knew he was too heavy, but at the moment couldn't summon the will to care. Or to move. Her arms wrapped around him so sweetly that for a moment, just a moment, he found surcease from the doubts that chased his every waking hour.

CHAPTER THIRTEEN

FOR THE FIRST TIME that she could remember, Vivian woke up with a hot, hard, male body wrapped around her. Sunlight was just beginning to filter in through the crack in her drapes and when she turned her head, she found Rafael was still asleep.

His eyes were closed, his tough mouth relaxed, and she realized he looked more vulnerable than she'd ever seen him. She ran a palm over the rough stubble of his jaw and simply enjoyed the feeling of being next to him. Being with him.

Last night had been… She stopped, unable to find the words to describe it. It had been incredible, she decided. Wonderful, magnificent, amazing. Not that she'd had a lot to compare it to, as she'd had only two lovers in her life, and both had been chosen more for their unthreatening, soothing manners than for their sexual prowess. But a girl knew quality when she found it, even if it was packaged differently than what she was used to.

Because while being with Rafael had been a lot of things—wild, fierce, emotional—the two things it hadn't been were unthreatening and soothing. She'd never been backed against a wall before, never had a man look at her like she was his whole world.

He made her vulnerable in a way that worried her. When he made love to her he paid attention to everything, every shift in breathing, every squirm, every sigh, until he knew her body as well as she did.

She still wasn't sure how she felt about that.

She tried not to let it go to her head, tried to convince herself that it was just the sex that had her feeling so in tune with him, but her heart didn't want to listen, and she cuddled closer to Rafael. Smoothed a hand over his brow. Dropped a kiss on his soft, relaxed lips. And hoped, desperately, that she wasn't making the worst mistake of her life. If this turned out badly, she didn't think she'd ever be able to open herself up again. Didn't think she'd ever be able to trust again. She was already taking a terrible risk, trying to believe him about his past. If it turned out she was wrong, she didn't know if she'd ever be able to forgive herself. Or him.

He stirred beneath her, stretched, and then his eyes popped open as if he'd just realized whose bed he was in. Her heartbeat started racing and she held her breath, waiting to see how he reacted to being with her as daylight slowly streamed through the window.

But he only smiled and wrapped one big hand around the back of her neck. "Good morning," he murmured as he drew her to him.

"Good morning." She started to ask if he wanted breakfast, to tell him he could use the shower first. To say any number of things, but then his lips found hers and she was lost, any and all words flying right out of her head.

As she sank into him, Vivian realized this kiss was different than any that had come before. Even through her whirling head and pounding heart, she felt the tenderness in the kiss. The sweetness. The belonging.

This wasn't the kiss of a couple of careless nights, or even a one- or two-week relationship. This was the kiss of a lover who cared about her, who wanted the best for her. Who wanted *her.* Relief swept through her, along with a warm rush that felt a lot like love, and she gave herself over to the kiss. To her lover.

To Rafael.

It was one of the hardest things she'd ever done—deliberately choosing to be vulnerable to him—but he'd been completely honest with her. She couldn't be anything else with him, couldn't hold back and hope he wouldn't notice.

With a soft groan, he rolled over so that he was on top of her. "What time do you have to be in court?" he murmured as he trailed his lips down her throat.

For long seconds, she couldn't think, only reveled in the feel of his lips moving slowly over her body.

"Vivian?" he prompted when she didn't answer. She was glad to hear in his voice the stress his restraint was costing him. It would have been awful to feel this open without knowing that he was as moved by her as she was by him.

"What?" she gasped, arching beneath him as his mouth did something truly wicked to the curve of her shoulder.

"Court?" he reminded her, and moved even lower. His lips skimmed over her breast and she squirmed, looked at the clock in desperation. Then smiled—it was only six-thirty.

"I've got three hours before I have to leave," she whispered.

She felt his mouth curve into a wicked smile against her breast. "That just might be enough time."

THREE AND A HALF HOURS later, Vivian battled her way through a throng of reporters on her way up the courthouse steps to the juvenile courtroom of Judge Alyssa Chambers. Vivian's heart was beating heavily as she issued a string of "No comment," her already taut nerves stretching to the breaking point as she nearly tripped over a photographer.

"Come on, guys. Give me a break. I'll have a statement for you later, I promise."

She might as well have been talking to the wall for all the attention they paid her. The butterflies in her stomach grew bigger at the thought. She had to win today, or Diego would once again hang in the court of public opinion. After the news broadcast she and Rafael had caught earlier that morning, she knew none of them could afford that.

The reporter had smiled smugly at the camera right before two pictures from the case flashed across the screen. They were bloody images of Esme hacked to death, and would have gotten the station in huge trouble for showing them—if they hadn't already been leaked on the Internet. The station had followed the pictures with the news that the boy accused of these crimes was now trying to get his case moved out of adult court to the juvenile system.

All hell had broken loose, and when Vivian called the
SFPD to file a complaint, she'd been given the same
statement the reporters had—they were taking the investigation of the leaked photographs seriously and
would come out with a statement once they knew more.

Yeah, right. In the meantime, Rafael had had to hire
a security guard to watch Diego's hospital room, to keep
away the angry mob of people trying to crucify him.

It had been a hell of a morning.

But she had to put all that aside and concentrate on
the case. She knew Judge Chambers casually, had
spoken with her numerous times at various fundraisers
through the years and had always been impressed by
how sharp and compassionate she was. Vivian had been
thrilled when she'd pulled her for Diego's hearing,
hoping that just maybe the kid would get a fair shake.

But hope wasn't enough. She had to win here today
and get Diego's case transferred to juvenile court or
they were in trouble. With all the press, she was seriously beginning to doubt if she had a chance of finding
twelve impartial jurors to try him in adult court.

Having only fifteen minutes to make her case wasn't
making her feel any better. Judge Chambers had sche-
duled half an hour on the docket for this preliminary
hearing, which meant Vivian had to hit the highlights.

On the positive side, her opposition was working
under the same circumstances.

As court was called to order, she risked a glance at
the prosecutor sitting at the table next to her. Assistant
D.A. Gallagher was known for his tough attitude and
unwillingness to plea-bargain. She'd never run up

against him in a courtroom, but a couple of her friends had and he'd been merciless.

That he was also known for his aspirations to the bench made things worse. The publicity surrounding this case was just the sort that might get him there—if he won.

"Ms. Wentworth." The judge's smooth, cultured tones filled the courthouse. "I understand that your client is still in the hospital, following a particularly brutal attack."

"Yes, Your Honor, he is."

"Do we need to reschedule? I checked before I came in and I have an opening in three weeks if that would give him enough time to heal."

"I believe we can proceed, Your Honor, if it's all right with you. I think we'd all like to know exactly what we need to be prepared for."

The judge studied her for a few seconds and then cleared her throat. "All right, then. Let's go ahead."

She turned to the prosecutor. "Mr. Gallagher, would you like to start us off?"

"Certainly, Your Honor." His voice was calm, relaxed, but Vivian had the feeling she had rattled him with her request to keep going. She'd bet a month's salary that he'd come in here prepared for her to reschedule, which was the number one reason she hadn't. With a prosecutor this shrewd, she'd take any and every opportunity she could to throw him off his game.

It quickly became obvious that she hadn't shaken him up enough, however, as he went about vilifying Diego.

"Your Honor, this crime is particularly heinous—the murder of a young girl and her unborn baby by the girl's trusted boyfriend. By the unborn baby's father. If ever there was a case to be tried in adult court, this is the one. Diego Sanchez was acting like an adult when he impregnated his girlfriend, and he was acting like an adult when he murdered her to get out of having a baby he didn't want.

"The M.E. has said there were no hesitation wounds on the body, no signs at all that Esme's killer wasn't completely reconciled to causing her death. In fact…"

Vivian took notes as Gallagher droned on about how moving Diego to juvenile court would be a travesty of justice. His voice was low, persuasive, as he fought for his case, and the knot in her stomach grew. Her one saving grace was that his arguments, while sound, were unoriginal, and she'd prepared for each and every one of them.

When it was her turn to speak, she took a couple of deep breaths and prepared for the argument of her life. "Your Honor, Diego is sixteen years old—well within the age bracket to be tried in juvenile court in California. And while I know the D.A. is convinced this case belongs in adult criminal court, I don't understand his rationale.

"The juvenile court system is set up specifically for cases like Diego's. He's a good kid, with a good record. He's never been in trouble at school—even after his mother died of cancer. He's never been involved with a gang or drugs or any other kind of street violence that might justify an adult trial."

She glanced at her notes. "In San Diego vs. K.M.P., the state Supreme Court says very clearly that juvenile court is the last bastion of defense against a generation of lost youth. As such, every effort should be made to keep a minor in the juvenile court system unless there are irrefutable grounds to try him as an adult.

"Heniousness of the crime, as Mr. Gallagher argues, is not enough grounds. The court set up three criteria that must be met before the juvenile system is allowed to wash its hands of the youth. First, he must be deemed unfit for rehabilitation because of life experiences or repeated patterns of behavior. Yes, Diego's had a rough life, but he's managed to rise above that again and again. He has no repeated pattern of behavior, no record of escalating crimes. This case—with its less than sturdy evidence—is the only crime this child has ever had to stand trial for. So the first burden of the state hasn't been met.

"Second, he must be evaluated by a psychologist who determines that he knowingly and willingly committed the crime. The prosecution has made no effort to have Diego evaluated—the only psychologist he has seen is the one the defense provided, and Dr. Stuart's report says the exact opposite."

"Do I have a copy of this report, Ms. Wentworth?"

"You do, Your Honor." When the judge gestured for her to continue, Vivian said, "And finally, it must be deemed in the juvenile's best interest to be tried in adult court. While some cases—and some defendants— would definitely benefit from having their day in adult court, Diego's case is clearly not one of them. Due to the volatile nature of this case, finding an impartial jury will be almost impossible. Photos have been leaked, reporters are following every development of the case, and between the police department's statements and those from the D.A.'s office, the public has been whipped into a frenzy against my client.

"As you know, Diego has already been severely beaten and the perpetrators are still at large. The teen center where he works has been vandalized in relation to this case. The system in place to keep Diego safe is failing, and it is up to this court to keep it from breaking down completely.

"From the moment he was arrested, Diego has been treated like an adult, and it hasn't worked for him so far. The police questioned him without a lawyer, parent or legal guardian present. They kept him in an interrogation room for seven hours, refusing to allow him to rest or use the bathroom. They went out of their way to treat him like a violent, adult offender when he's never been convicted—or even accused—of any crime.

"In Smith vs. the State of New Jersey, the Supreme Court ruled that juveniles must be protected by rules above and beyond adult offenders. They must not be questioned on their own. The police must not use interrogation techniques on them that the court deems 'threatening'—such as isolation, exhaustion, physical threats or emotional cruelty. The officers threatened to 'make his life miserable' and 'kick his ass' if he didn't confess. They even went so far as to tell him they would drop him off in front of the victim's house and 'let her brothers get a crack at him.'" Vivian paused, went over her last argument in her head and prayed that it was good enough to save Diego.

"Diego is a good kid who meets none of the criteria for adult court. The police have little evidence against him, and what they do have is far from conclusive—a statement from a half-blind neighbor and his DNA at the crime scene and in the victim's body. She was his girl-friend of two years and pregnant with his child, so the fact that they had sex sometime close to her death is per-fectly understandable. Diego has already suffered more than any child should have to. To move his case to adult criminal court is to allow the further victimization of my client, who, with the deaths of Esme and his unborn child, has already lost more than anyone should have to."

Vivian's legs were trembling by the time she'd finished her opening statement. It had been years since she'd been forced to make an argument in criminal court, and it was a whole different ball game than divorce court, especially since she'd come to care so much for Diego.

More than a little nervous, she studied the judge's face for any hint of which side she was leaning toward. Usually Vivian was pretty good at determining that, but Judge Chambers played things extremely close to the vest, and Vivian had absolutely no idea what the woman was thinking. The tense posture of the prosecutor implied that he felt exactly the same way.

"All right. Thank you both. I'll have a decision this afternoon, so why don't we plan on meeting back here at three-fifteen." She rose unexpectedly, which had both lawyers scrambling to their feet. "I'll see you then."

RAFAEL WAS LEADING A MATH study group when Vivian breezed through the front door of the center.

"We did it, Rafael!" she cried as she threw her arms around him. "The judge agreed to try Diego as a minor!"

For a moment, he was frozen as he tried to make sense of her words. Surely he hadn't heard correctly. Surely she hadn't just said—

"Rafael, did you hear me?" she all but crowed. "Diego's case is being transferred to *juvenile court.*"

A couple of the kids in the rec room cheered and their excited voices finally snapped him out of his disbelieving stupor. Grabbing Vivian's elbow, he propelled her down the hallway to his apartment and away from prying ears.

"How?" he demanded. "How did you do it? I honestly didn't think you had a chance in hell."

"Court precedents. Barnes and Turner's mishandling of the case. We also got a sympathetic judge, which always helps. When she gave her decision, she talked about how she wasn't ready to throw a kid away without knowing why. Are you ready for the best part?"

"Yes, of course." He felt his palms grow wet as he waited, unsure of what could be better than the news she'd already delivered. He couldn't wait to tell Diego. Couldn't wait to sweep Vivian up in his arms and thank her for everything she'd already done.

"She flat out told the D.A. that she wasn't impressed with the evidence, that at this point it seemed more flash than substance." Vivian paused for a breath. "Can you believe that? She's ripe for a dismissal motion, which I'm going to be drafting tonight. Of course, she said those things to give the D.A. a warning. He's going to be scrabbling for evidence in the next few days, looking for something absolute to put Diego away with."

"He's not going to find it."

"No, but that doesn't mean he's not going to be shaking a bunch of trees, much like we are. So get prepared, and get Diego ready."

"For what?"

"I'd be shocked if Turner didn't try to hassle him again, all in the guise of investigating the beating, of course. Plus, with everything going on in the press, it's going to be really dangerous for him for a while."

"I won't let Turner near him."

"Good."

Rafael pulled her into his arms, kissed her thoroughly. "Thank you so much for everything you've done for Diego. For me."

Her laugh was light, happy. "Don't thank me yet—we still have a trial to get through."

"Yeah, but you've evened the playing field."

"I sure did." Her voice was ripe with satisfaction. "And now I'm going for a home run."

He laughed. "Touchdown."

"What?"

"You're mixing your metaphors. When you're talking about a playing field, you're going for a touchdown."

"Whatever!" She giggled, sounding happier than he'd ever heard her. "Touchdown, home run, goal—they're all the same as long as I can keep Diego out of jail.

"But I've got to get back to the office. I have a client coming in at four-thirty. I should have called, but I wanted to tell you in person."

"I'm glad you did." He lowered his mouth, kissed her again.

"Me, too." It was her turn to kiss him. "But I really do

have to go. I'll come by in a couple hours and we'll celebrate. Pick up some ice cream or something and bring it to Diego at the hospital. Maybe this will cheer him up."

She was gone with another quick kiss and a wave, and Rafael was left staring after her like a lovesick fool, which completely freaked him out.

Last night had been the best of his life. Vivian was an incredible lover, the best he'd ever had. And the fact that she was also a wonderful woman with a great capacity for giving to others was another huge plus.

He drained the beer he'd been holding in one long gulf and then shoved a hand through his hair as he tried to sort out his mixed-up feelings. She was the perfect woman for him but he wasn't sure if he was ready for her. Wasn't sure if he could let her in.

Call him old-fashioned, call him narrow-minded, but he just couldn't get his mind around her money any more than he could deal with her being a part of the cultured elite he'd run up against with Jacquelyn. He'd already let Vivian in further than he'd planned, already trusted her with more of himself than he'd given another woman. But was it going to be enough?

Sure, she'd seemed fine with his parents—the other night she'd seemed to be having a great time with his friends and family—but that didn't mean she wanted to bring him into her own rarefied world. Jacquelyn had been content to go places with him, too, as long as no one she knew was going to be there.

As long as she didn't have to explain him to her daddy.

But Vivian wasn't like that, Rafael told himself. She wasn't cold or heartless or any of the other things Jacquelyn had been. She was smart and strong, and she stood by what she believed in. He only hoped it would be enough.

But wishing wasn't going to get him anywhere. When he added everything together, he couldn't get around the feeling that things were about to explode. Trust didn't come easy to him, and how was he supposed to trust her when she couldn't give him the benefit of the doubt?

They were caught in a vicious cycle, and he had no idea how they could get beyond it.

Furious, miserable and more confused than he'd been since the cops had shown up at his door all those years ago, Rafael reached for the phone to call Diego. Maybe delivering the good news would put him in a better frame of mind.

CHAPTER FOURTEEN

VIVIAN SMILED when she pulled into the small parking area behind Helping Hands and saw Rafael waiting for her. She hoped he didn't have anything planned for the evening, because she wanted to celebrate. She figured they'd stop by Diego's hospital room with dinner, and then maybe she'd talk Rafael into taking her dancing. Normally she wasn't big on the whole club scene, but she was so revved from her victory at work that she needed a way to burn off the excess energy.

Of course, if Rafael wanted to stay in to burn off that energy, then who was she to argue? She climbed out of the car with a big grin on her face, but the second she saw his face she faltered. "What is it?" she asked as she rushed to him. "What's wrong?"

"Diego's missing again."

"What do you mean, he's missing? You hired someone to guard him in the hospital."

"Yeah, well, I forgot to tell him to guard Diego from himself. The kid ripped out his IV and basically made a run for it during his afternoon walk." Rafael glanced past her. "So now he's out there alone, unprotected.

What if the cops find him before we do? What if Esme's brothers do?"

"Where do we start searching for him?"

The look he shot her was dark and distant and so reminiscent of the old Rafael that it had panic skating down her spine. "We start by you going home. I know the neighborhood. If he's here, I'll find him."

"That's the most ridiculous thing I've ever heard. You can't do this alone!"

"And I won't do it with you, so just go home. You're wasting time I could be using to find Diego."

Hurt shot through her. She tried to tell herself that he was just upset about Diego, that he didn't mean for things to come out the way they sounded, but even as she told herself that, she knew it wasn't the truth. Sucking in a breath she asked, "Why are you doing this? Why are you being like this?"

For a moment she thought she saw a flash in Rafael's eyes, but it was gone before she could figure out what it was. Pain? Derision? Fury? She didn't know, any more than she knew why he was pushing her away, when not so long ago he'd sounded so incredibly loving.

But she wasn't going to stand for it, wasn't going to put up with him throwing walls between them. Not now when she'd finally found someone she could connect with. Not now when a young boy desperately needed their help.

Clearing her throat, she straightened her shoulders and pushed the hurt to the back of her mind. She'd examine it later.

"Have you called his friends?" she demanded as she

walked past Rafael into the welcoming warmth of the teen center. "Have you talked to his father? Have you asked around to see if any of the kids here have seen him? With his bruises and broken bones, he's not exactly inconspicuous."

"What are you doing?" Rafael followed her down the hallway. "I told you I would handle this."

"And I told you that was ridiculous. There's no way I'm going to go hide at home while you deal with the hard stuff, so get over it, tough guy, and tell me what you want me to do."

Rafael stared at her for long seconds, his eyes blacker than she had ever seen them. But he must have come to some sort of a decision because he finally nodded toward the rec room. "Ask the kids if they've heard from him, while I call Diego's father. Hopefully something will pop."

Unfortunately, nothing did, and ten minutes later they were back where they'd started—with absolutely nothing. Rafael stared out into the streets that were slowly beginning to darken. "I have to go look for him."

"We'll split up—we can cover more ground that way."

"Are you kidding me?" he growled as he pulled her against him. "Do you really think I'm going to let you wander the Tenderloin alone? At night? We've already seen how well that works out for you."

For the first time since she'd arrived at the shelter, Vivian could feel a little of the tension inside of her ease. Pressed up against him, listening to his surly voice, she could almost pretend things were normal between them.

"Then let me come with you." He started to argue but she cut him off. "Please, don't tell me to go home again. It will just make me angry and then we'll have to argue, and we don't have time for that right now."

"I don't think—"

"Don't think." She put a finger over his lips to quiet him, and then jumped when he nipped at it. "Now, is there anyone you can call to help us out? Anywhere you think we should start?"

"I've already called Miguel, Gabe and Jose. I e-mailed Diego's picture to my brothers. They're going to start at the north end and work their way south."

"So that means we'll start down near Market," she said with a grimace. "Way to call the good area there, Rafael."

"I never expected you to come with me."

"Yeah, well, that just means you're a lot stupider than I gave you credit for." She headed toward the front door. "Now let's go."

"Yes, ma'am." He grabbed a recent photo of Diego from the picture collage on the rec room's back wall before following her out into the street. They headed south at a fast clip, showing Diego's picture to everyone who would look, but when they got to Market they had nothing to show for it except for some inventive new curse words they'd picked up from people who hadn't wanted to be bothered.

"You know, there's no guarantee he's even here," she said as they started to comb though the small ethnic restaurants and secondhand stores that made up this part of the Tenderloin. "San Francisco's a big place."

"If he hasn't gotten picked up by the cops or anyone else, then he's definitely here. He doesn't know any-place else."

"And if he did?" she asked, voicing the fear that had been inside of her from the moment she'd first heard Diego had gone missing.

"If he did, then I don't know where to start or what to do. It's much better to hope that he's hiding some-where familiar."

"But you don't believe that." She kept pace with Rafael's measured strides easily, knew that despite the precariousness of the situation he was trying to make her comfortable.

"I don't know what to believe and I won't know until I find Diego."

They combed the streets for hours, until well past midnight, but no one admitted to seeing him. She had to believe they would have spoken up if they had; almost everyone knew Rafael by sight and were a lot more forthcoming because of it. Most people in the neighbor-hood had a lot of respect for Rafael, and it showed.

Tired, defeated, they walked up the alley that ran behind Helping Hands. Rafael had his arm around her shoulders and was bolstering Vivian. After the emo-tional roller coaster of the day she was more exhausted than she had imagined it possible to be.

All she wanted was a bed and a few hours of unin-terrupted sleep, but when Rafael stiffened beside her she had a sick feeling that she would get neither.

With a muttered curse, he shoved her behind him. "What's wrong?" She pushed at him, trying to see what had him so upset, but he used his height to his advantage and refused to let her look.

"Come on, we're going in the front door." Grabbing her arm, he forced her to turn and began half running, half carrying her down the alley.

"Rafael!" She tried to dig in her heels, but he just pulled harder. "What's going on?"

"I'm not sure yet."

"What kind of answer is that?" she demanded as she raced to keep up with him. It was either that or be dragged.

She heard an engine roar to life behind her, heard tires squeal as a car peeled out. She tried to turn, but Rafael's grip on her elbow was untenable. "Look out," he yelled as he yanked her in front of him.

As the car drew closer, the driver gunned the engine, and it wasn't until she glimpsed the headlights headed straight for them that she began to understand the situation.

By then, everything was happening in slow motion. She and Rafael were running, but for those few moments, as the car barreled down on them, it felt as if they were slogging through quicksand.

Part of her recognized that Rafael had positioned himself behind her to take the impact of the car, and she wanted to protest, to scream at him to take care of himself. But her vocal cords had frozen up and all she could do was silently pray.

At the last possible second the car swerved and missed them. They stopped dead, and watched in relief as it careened past them. But before she could register what was happening, someone leaned out the window.

Rafael cursed and tried to yank her behind him, but a series of quick pops sounded, followed by a searing pain in her left thigh. Her leg went out from under her and she hit the ground, hard.

"Rafael?" Her voice was shaky, so high-pitched it was almost unrecognizable to her. "What's happening?" She clutched at him with trembling hands.

He was already shrugging out of his T-shirt as he dropped to the ground beside her. "You've been shot."

To her everlasting shame, those were the last words she heard before she passed out.

RAFAEL DIALED 911 with one hand while he pressed his shirt to the wound on Vivian's leg with the other. He sure as hell hoped he was putting pressure on the right spot. All but one of the lights in the alley had been broken, and he couldn't see.

But he could feel the blood seeping from the wound—thick and warm, it coated his fingers and struck fear into his heart. He didn't think the shooter had hit an artery—the blood was flowing too slowly for that—but there was still a lot of it. More than he'd ever imagined possible.

His shirt slipped off her leg and he realized it was already saturated with blood. Damn it. Maybe he'd been wrong, maybe the bullet *had* hit an artery.

Where the hell was the 911 operator?

Just then an impersonal female voice came on the line, saying, "911."

"A woman's been shot in the alley behind 1055 Ellis Street. She's bleeding a lot and it's so dark I can't see how bad the injury is."

Part of him wanted to move Vivian, to pick her up and carry her inside the center, where she'd be safe. But the other half was falling back on the first-aid training he'd learned in his certification class each year, and he knew better than to move a shooting victim.

He continued to answer the operator's questions even as he felt beneath the T-shirt for a wound. He finally found one—big enough that he knew the bastards had been firing some pretty heavy-duty bullets. The intent hadn't been to wound. It had been to kill.

Finally, after what seemed like hours but had probably been only two or three minutes, he heard sirens in the distance. With each second that passed, they grew closer, and he found himself praying for them to hurry up with each breath he took.

"Vivian." He called her name, his voice hoarse with panic. She'd been out a good three or four minutes and showed no signs of coming around. He had no idea if she'd simply passed out at the idea of being shot or if the loss of blood had caused it. The first seemed completely out of character, and it was too dark to see whether the second was a viable conclusion.

Damn those bastards. He'd give anything to go back ten minutes and take the turn onto Ellis instead of continuing into this godforsaken alley.

He'd known within seconds of stepping down it that something wasn't right, but he'd been so wrapped up in his worry over Diego and his feelings for Vivian that he hadn't figured out what it was until too late. Hadn't been able to register that the alley he usually kept lit up like the Fourth of July was entirely too dark.

"Come on, Vivian, talk to me." He reached up with the hand that still clutched his cell phone, and stroked his fingers softly down her face. "Sweetheart, please, let me see those gorgeous eyes of yours. Open up and look at me. Vivian, please."

The sirens were very loud now and he gave thanks for the surprisingly quick response. Shootings in the Tenderloin had grown common enough that on busy nights it took longer than it should to get help.

He looked up just in time to see an ambulance and two police cars turn into the alley. *Thank God.* Between their headlights and the red and blue strobe lights that flashed on their roofs, he got his first good look at Vivian since they'd turned into the alley.

What he saw was far from reassuring. She was pale—paler than he'd ever seen her—and blood was everywhere. On her jeans, on him, on the ground around them, and he cursed himself as the paramedics pushed him to the side. He'd thought he was protecting her, thought that the threat was from the car itself, when the bastards had had something else planned all along.

He should have known something like this was coming, should have anticipated the attack after Vivian had succeeded in getting the case moved to juvenile court. Should have protected her better.

"Did he hit an artery?" he demanded as the paramedics started to work on her. "She's lost a lot of blood."

"Let them do their work, Rafa." A heavy hand fell on his shoulder, and he glanced up to find Jose and his brothers standing next to him. It seemed like days since he'd talked to them, instead of only a few hours. Seemed like months since he'd asked Jose to scare the shit out of Nacho and his friends after they'd attacked Vivian, instead of a little more than a week.

As he watched the blood slowly leak from his lover's body, Rafael couldn't help resenting the fact that he'd let Nacho go with a warning. He'd thought he'd been protecting Vivian on the street that day, thought he'd been protecting a couple of teenage boys who didn't know any better than to act like animals.

But that hadn't been the case—he knew that now. Just as he knew that he was at fault. He was the one who had placed Vivian in this situation, and he was the one who had let her get hurt, who had stood by as she was threatened again and again.

No more. He was done with it. He'd thought that watching her fall after the bullet struck her was the most painful experience of his life. Even worse than being accused of rape. Even worse than going to prison for a crime he hadn't committed.

He'd been wrong. Watching the car drive away, getting a good look at the kid wielding the gun, had been worse. Because as he stared into Nacho's smug, high-as-a-kite eyes, he'd realized something else. He'd had it within his power to stop this all those days ago and he hadn't done it.

He'd been so blinded by his past—and his desire to keep innocent kids out of jail—that he'd let one who was far from innocent get away with harassment and assault, and now it appeared he had escalated to attempted murder. That Rafael had thought Nacho and his friends were harmless didn't matter. Nothing mattered except that Vivian and Diego were the ones paying the price for his stupidity.

"So, man, I know we can talk about this later." Jose's voice sound muffled, faraway, as Rafael looked down at the blood on his hands.

"Hey, man, are you with me?" Jose's hand on his shoulder got firmer, as if the cop was worried he might pass out or something.

"Is she going to be okay?" He watched the paramedics as they worked on Vivian—setting up an IV, trying to stop the bleeding. His whole world had narrowed down to this one moment, and he realized, with his typical bad timing, that he loved her.

That all the feelings that had been jumping around in him for days—admiration, desire, irritation at her for putting herself at risk, fear of rejection because of his past—added up to more than lust, more than friendship. He was in love with Vivian Wentworth.

He felt his knees go weak at his mistake, but he locked them in place.

"Hey, man." This time it was Miguel who got in his face. "Are you sure you didn't get hit? You don't look so good."

"I'm fine." He pushed his brother aside so he could keep Vivian in view. The paramedics had shifted her to a stretcher and were moving her to the ambulance with an urgency that didn't look good. He moved closer to the vehicle, angling himself to climb in when they were done getting her situated.

There was no way he was being left behind.

"I'm going with her," he told the paramedics as they started to close the bay doors.

"I need to talk to you about what happened." Jose's tone was adamant.

Ignoring him—and the hand his longtime friend held out to him—Rafael climbed into back of the ambulance. Vivian still hadn't come around.

"Pick up Nacho Soren." Their eyes locked. "I don't know who else was in the car, but he was the one with the gun."

Jose looked poleaxed. "Are you sure?"

Rafael nodded. "When he leaned out of the car to shoot her, he was right under that streetlamp." He pointed to the only one that still had a working bulb. "I saw one other kid and he looked familiar, but I don't know why. I'll let you know as soon as I figure it out."

Jose was already reaching for his radio when the ambulance doors closed. Desperate, furious, terrified, Rafael looked over at the paramedics and asked the only question that mattered. "Is she going to be all right?"

CHAPTER FIFTEEN

VIVIAN WOKE UP with the mother of all headaches and a stomach that was far from steady. Her leg was on fire and the rest of her body didn't feel much better. The events of the previous night rushed by—the shooting, waking up in the back of an ambulance with two paramedics and Rafael hovering over her, the doctors talking about stitches, a bad flesh wound and an overnight stay at the hospital.

Hospital… Her eyes popped open as she realized where she was—and how much time had been wasted. "Diego?" She tried to sit up, but she'd moved too quickly and the whole room began to spin.

"Shh." Rafael leaned over her, stroking a hand down the side of her face. "You're fine," he murmured. "You're in the hospital."

"I know where I am," she croaked, still trying to sit up, but taking it much slower this time.

Rafael pushed her back on the pillow, but when she started to protest he pressed the button to raise the head of the bed. "Do you want some water?" he asked. "They've been pumping you full of fluids—" he nodded at the IV attached to her right hand "—but they told me you'd be thirsty when you woke up."

She nodded, grateful for the chance to get the frog out of her throat, if for no other reason than being able to speak and be heard. He held a small hospital cup out with a straw and she began to drink thirstily.

"Take it easy," he said. "They gave you morphine and you don't want to get sick."

She nodded, but took a couple extra pulls on the straw before she laid her head back against the bed. Then she took a little while just to look at Rafael.

"Are you all right?" she asked.

His bark of laughter was anything but amused. "I think that's supposed to be my line." He'd put the cup back on the table and had clasped her hand in both of his while his fingers caressed her wrist.

"You don't look very good," she continued, which was pretty much the understatement of the year. He looked as if he'd aged five years overnight. The lines in his face were deeper and his eyes were shadowed. Plus he looked absolutely exhausted.

"I've had a rough night."

Fear clutched at her stomach, and the water she'd just drank threatened to come back up. "Diego—"

"We're still looking for him. But I was referring to you getting shot."

"Oh. That."

"Yes, that." His mouth was bracketed with pain when he leaned forward and rested his head on the side of her bed.

He still had a grip on her left hand, so she reached over with her right—IV and all—and stroked his hair. It felt as good as ever underneath her fingers—cool and silky and sexier than hair had a right to be.

Although she could remember parts of what happened last night, the details were hazy, as if she was looking at them from far away. She was smart enough to know it was the painkillers that were messing with her memory and gave everything an unreal quality.

Everything, that is, but Rafael. Through it all she'd felt his larger than life presence beside her, not getting in the way, but absolutely refusing to leave her alone to face the fear and pain. She remembered him holding her hand, whispering softly in her ear until the emergency room doctor kicked him out.

Rafael had saved her sanity along with her life, and she was incredibly grateful.

When he lifted his head, his eyes were damp and she felt her heart melt in her chest. "I'm fine," she told him as she squeezed one big hand between both of hers.

His jaw clenched and he looked away. His thoughts were so heavy she could almost see him beating himself up over something that was not his fault. She'd opened her mouth to tell him that he couldn't blame himself for what had happened when a familiar voice drifted down the hallway.

"Where is she? Where's her room?"

Stiffening in shock, she pulled away from Rafael and smoothed an absent hand down her hair. "What is my mother doing here?"

He looked at Vivian as if she was insane. "Once we got you settled up here, I called Richard, who promised to contact your family. They—"

Whatever he was going to say was lost forever as Lillian and Stephen Wentworth swept into the room.

"Oh, my God. Look at you."

"I'm fine, Mom. It looks worse than it is."

"You're patently not fine." Her mother's strident voice filled the room as she walked over and brushed a kiss on Vivian's cheek. "You were shot! I told you that pro bono work was going to get you in trouble one day, didn't I, Stephen?"

She turned to her husband, but he was too busy staring at Vivian to answer.

"I'm fine, Dad," she said, hoping to allay the concern she saw in his eyes. He nodded, but the look didn't change—and he didn't come any closer to her.

"Well, I hope now you'll quit your work for that terrible woman's shelter," Lillian went on, oblivious as usual to the undercurrents in the room. As the farce continued, Vivian couldn't help wondering if her mother had broken her own rules and already started on the day's quota of drinks.

"This had nothing to do with the woman's shelter, Mom. I was just in the wrong place at the wrong time."

"Yes, but why were you there?" her mother demanded. "In the Tenderloin, for heaven's sake? That place is filled with barbarians!"

Vivian stiffened and looked at Rafael, but he seemed too bemused by her mother, with her high-end suit, perfectly coiffed hair, pearls and obvious insanity, to be offended.

Lillian followed Vivian's gaze and for the first time seemed to notice Rafael sitting next to her daughter. "Are you the doctor?" she asked as she took in the scrubs the hospital had given him so he could change out of the bloodstained clothes he'd been wearing.

"No." He started as if surprised anyone could mistake him for a medical professional. "I'm…" He paused, obviously searching for a way to describe their relationship. He finally settled on one that was only a little bit of the truth. "I'm Rafael Cardoza, a friend of Vivian's. She was with me when she got shot."

"Are you telling me that *you* are responsible for my daughter being in that part of town?" Lillian asked, her mouth curled in a moue of distaste as her eyes lingered on the earring in his ear. Vivian couldn't help wondering what her reaction would be if she could see the black band tattooed around Rafael's upper biceps—it really was too bad the scrubs covered it.

"I am, yes."

"He is *not*." Her voice was still weaker than she would have liked, but Vivian worked hard to put as much force behind the statement as she could. "I was there because I wanted to be."

Stephen shot her a quick look before interrupting in his best doctor voice, "Let's everyone just calm down, all right?" He extended a hand to Rafael. "I'm Stephen Wentworth and this is my wife, Lillian."

Rafael smiled warmly, but she could see the unease in his eyes, especially as he glanced at her mother, who was obviously not happy to meet him. But Stephen had already picked up her chart at the end of the bed and was going over it carefully.

"Dad, is that really necessary?"

The look he gave her was surprisingly steely. "You

were just shot. As there's no doctor around to ask at the moment—" he glanced pointedly at Rafael "—then, yes, it is necessary."

"My father is a doctor," Vivian explained to Rafael. "He retired three years ago, but he doesn't seem to remember that."

"I remember it just fine, young lady. It says here that the bullet tore away a good-size chunk of flesh, nicked an artery." He looked at the scrubs Rafael was wearing in a whole new way, as if he had suddenly realized just how much blood Rafael must have been covered in.

"Oh, my God!" One beautifully manicured hand flew to Lillian's mouth. "You really could have died. What will people think?"

"I'm fine, Mom. Dad. Rafael called 911 and took care of me until the paramedics could get there."

Her mother ignored her. "So, Rafael? What were you and my daughter doing in that area of town in the middle of the night?" Lillian pinned him with a glare so intense that Vivian reconsidered her thoughts about her mother's sobriety. "It doesn't seem like a place *friends* would hang out."

"Lillian, your daughter has just been shot. Do you think maybe this could wait until later?" Stephen's authoritative voice cut the room like a knife, shutting her mother down instantly, and Vivian couldn't help staring at him in surprise. She'd only heard that tone from him a couple of times in her life, and never had it been directed at her mother.

"Of course." She turned to Vivian with a concerned smile that was so motherly Vivian had a hard time keeping herself from laughing. Or crying. "I've just been so worried about you." She moved to the left side of the bed, effectively shutting Rafael out of the picture.

It must have been the last straw for Rafael because he eased to his feet. "I should probably be going."

"No, Rafael—"

She started to protest, but he cut her off by leaning down and kissing her cheek. While he was there, he whispered, "I'll come by later. I think I'm upsetting your mother, and she doesn't need anything else to worry about right now." The way he said it made it seem as if he thought Lillian was one step away from a total break with reality, and Vivian barely suppressed a grin. Rafael was a lot better at getting a person's measure than he thought.

"Call me if you need me," he said as he pulled away.

"I'm sure that won't be necessary, Mr. Cardoza," her mother said in her frostiest tone. "I'll be here with Vivian until the doctor says we can take her home."

Vivian had to give Rafael credit when he only nodded sedately at her mother's pronouncement. She could see the gleam of amusement in his eyes as he noticed the sudden panic in her own.

"It was very nice to meet you, Lillian." He nodded to her father. "It's good to know Vivian's in such good hands."

Then he ducked out of the room before she could fire the water cup her mother had just handed her at his too-smug head.

RAFAEL'S AMUSEMENT FADED as soon as he'd slipped out of Vivian's room. *Those* were her parents? While it was nice to know Vivian would hold up well with age, if her mother was any indication, he found it hard to believe that a woman like *that* had raised someone as compassionate and good-hearted as Vivian.

He felt guilty ducking out and leaving her at her mother's tender mercies, but he was sick of being looked at as if he were something unpleasant stuck to the bottom of her shoe. It was hard enough for him to accept the fact that he'd fallen for Vivian—a woman whose background and money made him sweat—but to have to deal with her mother, who was so much like Jacquelyn she might have been her clone, was too much.

Especially when his nerves were so rattled. Digging his cell phone out of his pocket, he hit Jose's number.

"Where have you been?" Jose's voice came across loud and clear, despite the static on the line.

"With Vivian. Did you pick up Nacho?"

"Yeah, and he's not talking."

"Well, that's a big surprise. The kid's smarter than he looks."

"Yeah, but that's not the weird part."

"So what is?"

"He's lawyered up, tight as a drum. And not your typical scumbag lawyer, but one from a firm as fancy as your girl's."

"How's that possible? Where would he get that kind of money?"

"Exactly. Even stranger—I went round to pick up Danny and Ric, just to see if I could shake anything loose, and their mother hasn't seen them in two days."

"You know, Vivian and I think they're involved in what happened to their sister."

"I know. But I've been talking to Nacho's friends, and none of them are willing to admit that he even knows Esme's brothers. They say they've never seen them together, he's never talked to them, nothing."

"That doesn't mean anything."

"I know that, but I don't think they're lying. I talked to Esme's friends, too—same story. Nacho and his crew don't run with them."

"They're involved in this, Jose. I went to their house. I talked to them. Danny knows exactly what happened to his sister, though I'm not so sure about Ric."

"Well, can you come down to the station for a lineup? The lawyer's making noises about us not having any evidence to hold his client on, and I don't want to let him go. With the kind of money someone's shelling out for this lawyer, the second Nacho hits the street—"

"He'll be gone."

"Exactly."

"I'm on my way." Rafael punched the end call button harder than necessary as he tried to figure out what the hell was going on. He knew that in tying Nacho in with Ric and Danny, he had most of the pieces to the puzzle, but he couldn't seem to get them arranged to show the bigger picture. Maybe because the most important pieces were still missing.

It wasn't until he got down to the street that he realized he didn't have a ride. He stood there for a minute, shivering in the cold as he tried to decide what to do. He could call Gabriel to pick him up, but he wasn't in the mood for more rehashing.

Looking up and down the streets, he spotted the sign

of a major hotel a couple blocks away. Remembering that there was a BART station near there, he headed toward it at a fast clip. The train would probably get him home faster than a cab, anyway, and at the rate things were unraveling around him, he didn't have time to waste.

Diego was still missing. Vivian had been shot. Nacho was in custody, with a rich lawyer who wouldn't let him say a damn thing. And Rafael was seeing another suspect, one he was sure he'd seen before but whom he couldn't place to save his life, in his head. Oh, and he was crazy about a woman whose family left much to be desired. Things just didn't get much better than this.

He was half a block away from the BART station when he spotted one of Nacho's good friends coming up the station steps. The kid paused for a second as if trying to get his bearings, and then headed east.

For a second the sight of him in this neighborhood seemed so incongruous that Rafael just stopped in his tracks and stared, trying to decide if it was really Greg or if he was so tired and stressed out and furious that he was seeing things that weren't there. But he recognized the red backpack the kid carried as the same one he used to bring to the center. Add that to the fact that he was one of the boys who'd been hassling Vivian all those days ago when she'd tried to find her way to the community center, and Rafael wasn't about to let the opportunity pass by.

Maybe it was just a strange coincidence that Greg was here, maybe it wasn't. Either way, Rafael wanted to talk to him and find out what the hell Nacho was involved in. Picking up his pace, Rafael headed after the kid, making sure to keep his distance, as he was too tall to blend in well with the crowd.

He needn't have worried. The kid walked with his head down, looking neither left nor right. He was paying attention only to his destination, and Rafael had the feeling he could walk right up to him and the kid wouldn't even notice.

A couple of minutes later, Greg stopped at a local restaurant, and Rafael sped up so he could see if he was meeting someone. Nothing could have prepared him for what he saw when he ducked into the restaurant. Ignoring the hostess, he watched as Greg walked straight up to a table where Richard Stanley was sitting.

What the hell were Greg and Richard doing together? There was no legitimate reason they should be sitting at a table halfway between the Tenderloin and Nob Hill, in neutral territory where nobody should have recognized either of them.

Yet there they were. And when a third person joined the table—coming from what Rafael assumed was the restroom—the puzzle pieces finally fell into place. The second person he'd seen in the car, the same one he'd seen with Nacho in the taco shop last week, the one who was doing the gangster version of a handshake with Greg right now, was Richard's son. Rafael had met him at Richard's annual Christmas party last year, the same party he was supposed to be going to tonight.

If he remembered correctly, the kid's name was Thomas, and he was a chem major at Stanford. Rafael hadn't liked him the one time he met him—he'd been too spoiled, too insolent to impress him. He remembered thinking at the time that Richard needed to watch him. Wealthy and bored was not a good combination, especially when a youth had the sense of entitlement that this one had.

He recalled Thomas had reminded him too much of Jacquelyn and as he watched the three together, he couldn't help thinking that his instincts had been right on. This kid was trouble with a capital *T,* and it was obvious his father had finally figured that out.

Richard was uncomfortable, based on the stiff set of his body and the deep lines of his face. Thomas, however, seemed perfectly at home. He sprawled out in the booth, taking up more room than the other two men combined, and acting completely unconcerned. He was the only one who didn't look worried and Rafael hazarded a guess that his father had bought him out of more trouble in his life than any three people deserved.

Trouble like drugs.

Trouble like…murder?

Not wanting to let them out of his sight, but also not wanting to risk spooking them, Rafael ducked into a chair in the restaurant's waiting area that was out of Richard's line of sight, but still provided him a decent view of the table. Taking out his cell phone, he snapped a couple shots of Thomas, and then dialed Jose back.

"I thought you were on the way?" Jose barked into the phone.

"Yeah, well, I think I just stumbled on something a whole lot bigger than Nacho." Then he told Jose what he was looking at. The cop and his partner were out the door and on their way before Rafael had finished speaking.

That son of a bitch, was all Rafael could think as he stared at Richard. He'd been the one to stick Diego with a divorce attorney for a lawyer. Vivian had done a great job, but Richard couldn't have known that at the time. Rafael had called him for help and the bastard had been sabotaging him all along.

When Rafael had read the article the paper had run about Vivian a few days before, it had never occurred to him that Richard had had a personal agenda in assigning her to the case. That he'd been expecting her to fail.

But she hadn't, and the better she did with the case, the more dangerous Richard became. Getting Diego's case sent to juvenile court had obviously been the last blow. Richard had panicked at the thought of Diego getting off—which might force the cops to look for another suspect—and had Vivian shot.

Hell, yeah, the puzzle pieces were fitting together left and right, and the picture they made wasn't a pretty one. Rafael's best guess was that Thomas had a nice little side business going on—one that included supplying drugs. Whether he or his friends cooked them up in their chemistry lab he didn't know—and honestly didn't care.

But it was obvious, even from across the room, that the kid was a user. His eyes were so bloodshot Rafael could see them from where he was sitting. The way he kept wiping his nose and the weird little facial tic he had going on had him guessing that Thomas's trip to the bathroom had been to do a line or two of the hard stuff. Not enough to get high, but just enough to take the edge off.

But drug use wasn't enough. The million-dollar question was had he killed Esme? That his dad had worked to make sure Diego went down for the murder seemed to indicate that he had.

Why? Had her brothers gotten greedy on their portion of the profits? Maybe, but that just didn't ring true for Rafael. Rich kids like Thomas dabbled in this stuff because they thought it made them look cool, because they liked the adrenaline and the risk. Rafael hadn't met very many who had the guts to do murder because they were gypped a few dollars, especially since it was so rarely about the money to begin with.

Then why? Why kill Esme? Why—

"Rafa!" Jose and his partner, Sam, came through the door in an authoritative whirl. "What the hell's going on?"

"I'm not sure," he told them honestly. "But the blond kid over there was in the car with Nacho when he shot Vivian."

"Are you positive?"

"I am. His name is Thomas Stanley and his father sits on my board. It's why the kid looked so familiar to me when I saw him in the taco shop."

Jose muttered something under his breath, and though Rafael didn't catch the whole thing he was pretty sure it was something about rich kids and the mess they liked to make. It was nice to know he wasn't the only one feeling that way today.

But Thomas was more observant than they'd given him credit for, and the second Jose started across the restaurant's dining room, the kid bolted. Someone screamed, but it was over in a second, when Jose's partner, Sam, tackled the kid. Soon Thomas was being hauled out in handcuffs, while Richard and Greg got a police escort out of the restaurant. Richard was screaming to everyone who would listen about police brutality and who he was going to sue, and not even the five hundred bucks' worth of crank they pulled out of his son's pocket shut him up.

Rafael watched the whole scene with a kind of horrified bemusement. Then turned and walked toward the BART station as he wondered where they all were supposed to go from here.

CHAPTER SIXTEEN

WHEN RAFAEL FINALLY GOT back to the center, he found Diego sitting in the hallway outside his apartment. His back was braced against Rafael's door and he had a gun in his hands.

Adrenaline hit Rafael like a runaway bus as he registered what he was seeing. But he kept his voice calm, his gaze level as he said, "Are you all right, Diego? We've been looking all over for you."

Diego's face was tearstained as he looked up. "I couldn't stay in that room anymore, staring at the ceiling. I was going crazy. All I could think about was Esme and the baby and how much I missed them." He raised the hand with the gun and used the sleeve of his jacket to wipe his nose while Rafael had a quiet heart attack.

"What am I going to do without them?"

A million words came to mind, thousands of trite phrases that didn't mean anything. Looking at Diego, Rafael knew he couldn't use any of them. Sinking down on his haunches next to him, he said the only thing he knew was true. "I don't know, but we'll find a way."

"It hurts, Rafa. Like there's this great big hole inside

of me. Like, without Esme and the baby, I'm just a useless waste of space, like my dad."

"That's not true."

"Sure it is." He wiped his nose again. "Look at the mess I'm in. You and Vivian are working so hard to save me, and I don't even know if I want to be saved. What have I got to look forward to? Twenty-five years in jail instead of life? Or am I just going to waste away like my father—become a total *pendejo* that no one gives a shit about?

"He's drunk all the time, doesn't get out of bed most days. He didn't even come to her funeral!"

"I know, Diego." Rafael took a deep breath, tried to figure out the best way to reach the kid. "But things have changed since you left the hospital. A lot has happened. Vivian got your case transferred—"

"I don't care!" He lifted the gun nearer to his head "Don't you get it? I want to die."

"I know you do." Sweat slipped down Rafael's back and he started to shake as the muzzle of the gun got closer to Diego's temple. He wanted to reach out and grab it, to yank it away, but he was afraid to set Diego off.

"But you can't. Who's going to remember Esme if you die? Who's going to bring flowers to her grave?"

"You can."

"Diego, if you kill yourself, I guarantee you I will not be in any condition to bring anyone flowers."

Diego gave him a bemused look. "What does that mean?"

"You matter to me. You think if you off yourself I'm just going to go on my merry way and live my life?"

"You don't understand what it's like."

"So tell me about it. Tell me what it's like."

"It hurts so bad. I wake up every morning and the pain is worse than the day before. It just keeps getting worse and worse, like a cup that never fills up. I want it to go away. I just want it to end."

Tears were rolling down his face, but Diego didn't seem to notice. He just kept talking, breaking Rafael's heart with every word he said. "Sometimes I dream that she's still alive, you know. I hear the baby crying—I swear to God, Rafa, I hear him in my sleep, and when I wake up, just for a minute I think it's going to be okay. And then I remember…"

"It's going to be okay, Diego."

"How? How's it going to be okay when Esme's gone? I've got nobody, I've got nothing. She made me something, made me feel like I finally belonged to someone. Made me feel like I had a family.

"Now I'm back to the way things were before her, only it's worse. Because now I know what it can be like. Now I know what I should have. I don't want to live like this. I'm sorry, Rafa, but I don't." He put the gun against his temple.

"Diego, no! You matter to *me*."

"I'm sorry about the mess, Rafa." His hand trembled as he started to cock the gun. "Sorry about everythi—

Desperate and half convinced he was going to be too late, Rafael lashed out and hit Diego's hand with every ounce of strength he could muster. The gun flew out of his grip and hit the wall hard before falling to the floor between them.

Rafael grabbed it, shoved it far behind him.

Diego looked at him, bewildered, as the tears flowed freely down his face. "What'd you did that for, Rafa? Why'd you do that?"

"Because you're *my* family, Diego. And I'm not letting you go." He pulled the kid into his arms and held him while he sobbed.

Long minutes passed as Diego held on to him as if he was the only thing keeping the kid grounded, and Rafael held on just as tightly. He'd almost lost this kid who was like a son to him. Almost had to watch him die after Vivian had fought for him to live.

Rafael's heart was still beating triple time. The way he was feeling, Diego would be lucky if he let him go before his thirtieth birthday.

Eventually, though, the crying stopped and the boy raised tear-swollen eyes to Rafael. "I just miss her, you know? I really, really miss her."

"Of course you do. And with everything that's been going on, you've barely had a chance to mourn her. But that's going to change now."

"How?"

Rafael climbed to his feet, extended a hand to Diego, then pulled him up. Picking up the gun, he emptied it of bullets before opening the door to his apartment. "Come on in, and I'll tell you what I know."

VIVIAN STARED AT HER mother, sure that she had heard her wrong. "You did what?"

"I had Rafael investigated. I've only got the preliminary report in, but it's a doozy."

It had only been twelve hours since her mother had *met* Rafael, and most of the time she'd spent sitting next to Vivian's hospital bed. And while her mother had brought her back to her apartment—at her insistence— two hours earlier, Lillian had continued to hover so closely that Vivian was beginning to wish that the doctor hadn't reduced her pain meds. A little drug-induced oblivion would come in handy about now.

"You've been with me all afternoon. When on earth could you have done it? Why did you do it?"

"I called a friend who uses private detectives regularly. You remember Mitzy Graham, don't you? Anyway, she put me in touch with her guy, who—for a substantial fee—went to work right away. He's not done, by a long shot, but already he's gotten the goods."

Gotten the goods? Vivian stared at her mother in disbelief. Who talked like that? She tried to stand so that they could be on more equal ground, but her leg ached too badly to support her. "Why would you do that?"

"Because the man looks like a dirtbag, Vivian. I mean really, an earring? Long hair? And I swear I saw a glimpse of a tattoo."

"Rafael doesn't have a tattoo."

"Still, only teenagers and rock stars can get away with looking like he does, and believe me, Rafael Cardoza is neither."

"Would it be better if he looked like Brandon?" The words were out before she could stop them, and as her mother flinched, Vivian wished she could take them back. But damn it, her parents had all but handpicked Brandon for Merry, and he'd turned out to be a misogynistic, wife-beating rapist who drove her sister to suicide. How dare her mother complain about who Vivian chose?

"Don't you see, Vivian? Brandon had everything going for him and still he turned out to be dangerous. I don't want the same thing to happen to you that happened to your sister, and this Rafael seems to be cut from the same cloth.

"He's a convicted rapist, Vivian. He spent five years in jail for raping Jacquelyn Wesley—"

"Stop right there."

"You're too young to remember it, but I do. I used to play bridge with Jacquelyn's mother. That girl was brutalized. She walked around looking like a punching bag for weeks—black eyes, broken nose, the whole works."

"I said stop, Mother!"

"Denying it won't help." Her mother held out a folder. "It's all right there for you to see."

"I already know about it. He told me everything before things ever got serious between us."

"And you stayed with him?" Her mother was scandalized, not just pretending this time, but completely, totally horrified. "Why would you do that?"

"Because he told me he didn't do it and I believe him." It was the first time Vivian had said the words, the first time she'd allowed herself to totally believe them, and they felt good. There was no way Rafael was a rapist, no way he was anything like her sister's husband or any of the men Vivian saw or heard about down at the shelter.

He was big and gruff and had a temper, but he'd never once hurt her. He'd gone out of his way to keep her safe, to take care of her, and the man she knew—caring, compassionate, spending every penny he had to run a center for kids who didn't have anyone else to stick up for them—could never deliberately violate a woman the way her mother was saying Jacquelyn had been violated.

"That's the most ridiculous thing I've ever heard, Vivian." Her mother's voice continued to drone on. "Brandon was a good liar, too, despite growing up with all the advantages money could buy. This Rafael has almost nothing."

"Get out, Mom."

"What did you say?"

"I said get out. Get out, get out, get out!" Sitting here listening to her mother of all people talking about Brandon, when *she'd* been the one who had most stridently defended him, was almost more than Vivian could bear. After everything Brandon had done, to hear her mother say that Rafael was *worse,* was something Vivian absolutely couldn't tolerate.

"Did you hear me, Mother?"

Lillian was sitting on the couch with her mouth open as if she couldn't possibly comprehend what her daughter had said.

"Be reasonable, Vivian. You're injured. How will you take care of yourself?"

"I'm injured, not paralyzed. I'll figure things out." She sounded brave, and Vivian wasn't sure how honest she was being, but she'd be damned if she showed her insecurities to her mother. Lillian needed to go and she needed to go now, or Vivian just might call Security and make her go, which should make for a particularly warm Black-and-White Ball on New Year's Eve.

"I can't believe you're doing this!"

"I can't believe you so grossly invaded my privacy and Rafael's."

"I wanted to help you, Vivian."

"You didn't do it to help me. You did it to hurt me—to drive me away from someone I care about because he isn't good enough for you. But I'm not Merry, Mother. You can't run my life the way you tried to run hers."

"I was only trying to help."

"You were trying to control me. You don't like Rafael because of how he looks, so you did your best to discredit him. But if he'd looked like Brandon, if he'd been a good little banker, you would have given me your blessing and not cared if Rafael was the biggest bastard on earth."

She paused, got her breath back. Then said quietly, "Please go."

Her words must have finally sunk in because Lillian gathered her purse and headed for the front door.

"Take the report, too. I don't need it."

"Be reasonable, Vivian." The face Lillian turned on her was imploring, but Vivian hardened her heart to it.

"I've been reasonable. For my whole life I've been reasonable. I'm sick of being reasonable, Mother. Sick of catering to your moods and your prejudices and your inability to deal with things you don't want to know about."

Stopping in midtirade, Vivian buried her face in her hands and tried to breathe past the crushing lump in her chest. She wasn't going to change her mother, wouldn't even know how to go about trying, so why was she berating her for something that couldn't be helped? It was a waste of energy she couldn't currently afford.

"Look, Mother. I'm sorry I snapped. I know you meant well, but you're going to have to trust me on this. I love Rafael and I'm not going to turn my back on him because he doesn't come with a socially acceptable pedigree. Now, it's time for you to leave."

Head up, back straight, her mother finally did what Vivian asked. She left without a backward glance. And as the door closed behind her, Vivian didn't have a clue what she was supposed to do next.

CHAPTER SEVENTEEN

VIVIAN WOKE TO A LOUD pounding in her head. Disoriented as she was from the pain pill she'd taken before falling asleep, it took her a minute to figure out that someone was at the door.

"Vivian. Are you in there? Vivian?" Rafael said through the panel, sounding panicked.

"Yeah," she said, trying to struggle to her feet. Her leg burned like crazy, worse than before she'd taken the painkiller. How long had she been asleep, anyway? "Hold on," she called.

"It's Rafael, Vivian. Are you in there alone?"

"Give me a second."

A string of curses drifted through the door as she slowly hobbled across the room. Maybe she'd been a fool to turn down the crutches they'd offered her at the hospital, but she'd been afraid of falling flat on her face as she tried to use them.

Her drug-fuzzed brain had her struggling with a lock that a kindergartener could open. The second it clicked free, the door flew open and Rafael pushed his way in.

He swept her up and into his arms the second the door closed behind him. "What are you doing walking on that leg? Why are you here alone? Why didn't you call me?"

"My mother brought me home a couple of hours ago, but when she got on my nerves I begged her to leave so I could sleep. That's what I was doing when you got here—getting ready for bed."

"I'm sorry." He sat beside her and brushed a kiss over her forehead. Her traitorous heart beat faster, but she willed it not to respond. "I should have called you, but things went unbelievably crazy after I left the hospital."

"What happened? Did you find Diego?"

His face clouded. "Oh, yeah. When I got back to the center he was sitting in front of my door with a gun. He wanted to die, Vivian."

"Oh, no! Is he okay?"

Rafael sank against her, his head resting in the curve of her shoulder as he took long shuddering breaths. "For now. I called a friend of mine who's a counselor. I'd tried to get Diego to see her before, but he wouldn't have any part of it. This time I told him he doesn't get a choice."

"Good."

He shook his head. "It was unbelievable, Vivian. I was sure he was going to shoot himself, and I couldn't fathom what I was going to do without him."

"That must be what he feels like, having lost Esme and his son."

"Exactly. The poor kid—I can't imagine what he's been walking around with since they died. Oh, and there's more."

As he told her the story of what had happened, Vivian's stomach flipped over again and again as she stared at him in disbelief. "I used to babysit Thomas when they came to our house," she said hoarsely. "He was just a baby."

"Yeah, well, he's not a baby anymore, and he's in a world of trouble. Despite the fact that his father had him lawyered up, the kid's cocky enough that he just might give them a confession for Esme's murder. Jose seems to think it's a possibility, not that he's sure they'll need it. They found Esme's address in his wallet and he doesn't have any good excuse as to why it's there."

"Her brothers?" she asked, horrified at the thought.

"I think so."

"But how is that possible? Why would Thomas do this?"

"Too much money, not enough supervision." He shook his head sickly. "I don't know what makes a kid who has every advantage do something like that."

"So what happens now?"

"Now the police try to figure out which way is up. Richard has them so protected it'll be a miracle if one of them breaks, but I'm hoping Greg will. He doesn't strike me as having much backbone."

Vivian thought back to the kid who had watched Nacho attack her outside the community center, and had to agree. But still… "So does this mean Esme's brothers were involved, after all? Or that they weren't?"

"Jose's pulled them in for questioning, as well. Judging from their reactions when they saw Thomas Stanley behind bars, I'd say they knew he killed their sister. But I think the money and the drugs were more important to them—at least to Danny—than seeing their sister's killer punished."

"That's…"

"I know. Disgusting, right?" He pulled her against him and cradled her in his arms.

They stayed that way for a while, Rafael twirling a strand of her hair around his finger while she listened to the steady beat of his heart. Eventually her leg started to hurt too much for her to ignore, and she shifted, trying to find a more comfortable position.

"Do you need another pain pill?"

"I think so, but I hate them. They make me so drowsy."

"Better that than suffering. Where did your mom put them?"

"I think they're on the kitchen counter."

He kissed the top of her head. "I'll be right back."

He was as good as his word, quickly returning with a pill and a large glass of water. "So what happened to your mother?" he asked, settling down next to her again. "I thought she was supposed to be here taking care of you?"

"I kicked her out."

"Why?"

Vivian wasn't sure what she was supposed to say to that. Precious seconds ticked by as she tried to find a decent answer, but finally she just gave up. "She had you investigated."

"Excuse me?"

"She was upset when she found you in my hospital room, and she wanted to find something to make me break up with you."

"And she found it, didn't she? What'd she have to say about my rape conviction?"

"She wanted me to dump you."

"And that's why you kicked her out?" His voice was completely emotionless. He had withdrawn far from her despite the fact that he still sat next to her on the couch.

"I kicked her out because she was trying to control me, and I won't have that. She's entitled to her own prejudices, I suppose, but that doesn't mean she can try to foist them on me. I'll pick who I hang around with, and to hell with what she and my father think is best. It's not like they've got the best judgment in the world."

"You shouldn't have done that."

Of all the things she'd thought he might say, that was the least expected. "What do you mean? Of course I should have—I care about you. And she has no right to judge you. Especially since she's never bothered to have a real conversation with you."

"She's your mother. I don't want to come between you two."

"Give me a break. It's not like we're normally all warm and fuzzy, and you just got in the way. We've always had problems."

"Still." He shoved himself up from the couch. "If I've learned nothing else in the last couple of weeks, it's that family is everything. You don't give it up if you don't have to."

"Not everyone's family is like yours."

"I know that, but at the same time, you need whatever bonds you have. Diego nearly died because he lost those bonds."

"And Esme *did* die because of her family ties. There are all kinds of families, Rafael, and I don't want to be a part of one that's so cold and calculating. Not anymore."

"Yeah, well, what happens when you're not mad at your mom anymore."

"Excuse me?"

He walked over to the window, stared out at the storm-tossed ocean for what seemed like forever. "I won't come between you and your family."

"You aren't."

"Of course I am. And while you're okay with it now, what about next week, when it's Christmas?"

"My parents are going away for Christmas and leaving me here. Believe me, it won't bother me at all."

"Okay, what about your birthday then? Or when you get promoted to partner?"

"Yeah, well, I won't make partner anytime soon. This whole Richard debacle should make me persona non grata around the firm for a while."

"What's that supposed to mean? He's the one who assigned you the case so you could fail and he's the one who had you shot when you didn't. How is that your fault?"

"You obviously still have a lot to learn about how things work on my side of the tracks."

"That's my point. I don't fit in—and I never will. Your parents won't accept you being with me and there will come a time when you want them. I don't want you to ever feel like you had to choose between me and them."

"My mother made the choice."

"Don't you see? That makes it worse."

"No, it doesn't." She stood up, tried to limp over to him, but he was across the room in a second, settling her back on the sofa.

"Yes, it does. Vivian, if you do this, you'll come to resent me."

As his words finally sank in, the lightbulb clicked on. *He hadn't said it back.* She'd told him that she loved him, and he'd told *her* that she should make up with her mother. She'd been so caught up in her argument with her mother that she hadn't realized it until this very second.

Could she have been any more of a fool?

"That's what this is about, isn't it? This has nothing to do with my mother. You don't trust me."

"I didn't say that." He shoved his hands in his pockets, backed away.

"You didn't have to. One rich girl didn't stick by you, so why would another? We're all the same, right?"

"That's not what I mean."

"Sure it is. You've been saying it from the beginning, thinking it. But I thought we'd moved beyond the stereotypes. If I can believe you when you tell me you're not a rapist, why can't you believe that I love you? That I want to be with you? That I don't care what my parents or my friends or anyone else says about you? About us?"

"Come on, Vivian. It wouldn't work—you know that."

"No, *you* know that. You've always known it. Right, Rafael? You never expected this to work. So why did you start it? Why'd you take me out, let me meet your family? Why'd you make love to me like that if you never planned on sticking around?"

"You can't live your life torn between two different sides. It can't work."

"I'm not torn. You are."

"You're not being reasonable."

"Well, excuse me. So you want me to be rational? Fine." She limped over to the door and swung it open. And for the second time in twenty-four hours, she looked at someone she loved and told him to get out.

CHAPTER EIGHTEEN

FIVE DAYS LATER, Rafael sat with his family around his mother's Christmas tree, watching as everyone opened presents. Carolina's two girls were squealing in delight over their gifts from Santa, while Miguel's son was using his lightsaber to battle imaginary galactic forces of evil. Even Diego was getting into the spirit, fiddling with the MP3 player Rafael had bought him and loaded with his favorite songs.

And Rafael had never been more miserable in his whole damn life. Even the five years he'd spent in prison hadn't been this bad. At least then he'd had an ending in sight. A timetable he could mark off as each awful day passed.

Being without Vivian wasn't like that. Every day was an empty ache, one that had him going stir-crazy before the first week was up. And the knowledge that this was forever—that he would never be with her again—was nearly unbearable.

What had he done? The question haunted Rafael as it had every morning since he'd walked out of Vivian's apartment, working itself insidiously into his brain until it was all he could think about, all he could focus on.

When Vivian had told him that she loved him, he should have dropped down on his knees and thanked God for her. He should have at least wrapped his arms around her and told her that he felt the same way, that nothing else mattered but the two of them.

But he'd been stupid and had let his damn pride get in the way. Had let his fear of being hurt again stand between him and the only woman he'd ever loved. Was it possible for him to be a bigger *pendejo?*

It had messed with his head when she'd told him her mother knew about his rape conviction. All he could think about was the months and years Lillian Wentworth would look down her nose at him, thinking he was scum. Would work insidiously on Vivian, trying to get her to change her mind about him. It wasn't as though he didn't have enough strikes against him without the conviction.

But he'd forgotten something in all that. Forgotten that Vivian was the most steadfast person he'd ever met. She rarely faltered; she stood up for the things she believed in. If she loved him, of course she would stand up for him, too. She already had when she'd kicked her mother out. Had continued to do so when—after everything that had happened between them—she'd rushed a dismissal motion through the court so that Diego could be a free man by Christmas.

And what had Rafael done besides cower behind his misconceptions and fears? How had he showed her that he loved her, too? He hadn't. He'd been too busy worrying about the past to work on the future. As far as mistakes went, his was a doozy.

"Come on, Rafa. If you're going to be this miserable, you should just go get the girl." Michaela beaned him in the head with a bright red box. "You haven't opened one present, haven't done anything but mope. Man up and go tell your woman you screwed the pooch."

"How do you know he's the one who screwed up?" Miguel demanded. "She could have—"

"She didn't. Vivian's good people," Michaela said.

Great. What kind of idiot was he that his baby sister had figured out in one evening what he hadn't been able to get his mind around in three weeks? "She's right. I screwed up."

"So go fix it." His father smacked him on the back of the head. "You think love is all about fairy tales? Everyone screws up at one time or another. It's what you do about it afterward that makes all the difference."

His mother leaned over and planted a big kiss on her husband's mouth. "I couldn't have said it better myself, *mi novio.*" She raised an eyebrow at Rafael. "Why are you still here?"

"I'm not." He sprang up and headed for the door.

"Yo, bro."

"What?" he asked Gabriel, impatient to be on his way.

"Just a suggestion, but you might change out of the Santa Claus pj's before you go running after the love of your life."

VIVIAN SAT ON THE COUCH, staring at her lonely little Christmas tree and feeling absolutely miserable. Her leg still throbbed, she was coming down with a cold and she was alone on Christmas. Could she get any more pathetic?

Oh, yeah, and the man she loved had walked away from her five days ago, without a backward glance. Nope, she officially won the Most Pathetic award of the year.

She couldn't sleep, couldn't eat, could barely function. The only bright spots had been getting Diego's charges dropped and watching Richard get indicted for attempted murder in her shooting and conspiracy to commit murder after the fact in Esme's death. It turned out her boss had done a lot more than simply assign the wrong attorney to the job. As first Greg and then Nacho had broken, the whole story had come tumbling out.

Thomas had killed Esme in a PCP-fueled rage. When he'd woken up covered in blood, he'd enlisted his father's help, who had then worked to keep his son out of the investigation's spotlight. He'd paid Detective Turner to find a suspect that would roll over, and had had Thomas cough up the names of local thugs they could use to do their dirty work. He must have had a stroke when Rafael had called him for help with Diego's case, but he hadn't been able to say no. It would have looked strange if he'd refused to help one of the kids at the center he'd dedicated so much time to.

The press was having a field day, and Richard had been ruined. It almost made worthwhile Vivian's awful days as the focus of all that media scrutiny. Almost.

Slumping down on the sofa, she nursed her mug of eggnog and tried to convince herself that she was quite happy watching football games and eating a turkey sandwich.

When the knock sounded at her door, she ignored it at first. But whoever was there was persistent, and finally she dragged herself across the room and wrenched the door open, only to come face-to-face with Rafael.

He looked as upset as she felt.

"Merry Christmas," he said with a smile that didn't reach his eyes.

"Merry Christmas."

When he didn't say anything else, she asked, "What are you doing here?"

"Can I come in?"

"Of course." She stepped back, let him in.

"How's your leg?" he asked as he trailed her to the sofa.

"It hurts, but it's better than it was."

"I'm really sorry—"

"Please tell me you didn't come here to talk about me being shot."

"I didn't."

"Good." She gestured to her cup on the coffee table. "Do you want some eggnog?"

"No."

"Okay." She sank onto the sofa. "So what do you want?"

"You." He deliberately echoed her answer to his question of the week before.

"I'm sorry?" Her eyes darted to his.

"You're not the one who needs to apologize."

He paused for a minute. "I blew it, Vivian. I'm sorry. I screwed everything up. I was just scared and it gave me the excuse to turn away from you."

"What did you possibly have to be scared of?"

"You're everything I've ever wanted, Vivian, and was afraid to ask for. Everything I ever needed and didn't know *how* to ask for. So when you came into my life and made me fall in love with you, I kept looking for excuses to get out. I kept looking for a reason for us to fail. You had too much money, your world was too different from mine, I didn't want to get between you and your family.

"But they were all excuses, ways for me to put distance between us because I didn't trust my feelings—or yours."

"Why?" The word burst from her. "Love is rare—why would you want to just throw it away?"

"What happened with Jacquelyn screwed me up. Made me think that caring about someone made me vulnerable. Made me weak." He looked away. "I spent five years in prison for something I didn't do because I trusted a woman. I lost my freedom, lost who I was, almost lost my family because I was too embarrassed to reach out for them. I was worried about making the same mistake again."

"You thought I would do that to you."

"No, of course not. Not rationally. But letting my guard down, trusting anyone, isn't easy.

"But you changed all that. You made me feel alive for the first time in fifteen years. You made me understand that I could love someone and not lose who I'd become. Most of all, you taught me what it means to love another person so much that her happiness is more important than my own."

He looked her straight in the eye and said, in the dark, gruff voice she had come to adore, "I love you, Vivian, more than I can ever tell you. You've given me love and support and friendship and passion, and rolled it all up into one incredible package. I can't promise I'll never hurt you again, but I promise that I'll never walk away from you. I'll never again let my issues get in the way of what I feel for you."

Vivian watched him for long seconds, this brave, compassionate man who knew more about the ugly side of life than she ever would. If he was willing to take a risk, willing to love her, then how could she do anything else?

"I love you, Rafael. Sometimes I think I was born to love you."

"Good, because I *know* I was born to love you." He leaned forward until his lips just brushed hers.

She wrapped her arms around his neck and brought him in for a deeper kiss. "Just remember that after we've been married for thirty years."

"You want to *marry* me?"

"Well, of course I do." The shock on his face had her backtracking nervously. "Well, I mean only if that's what you want—"

"That doesn't sound like much of a marriage proposal. What happened to pledges of undying love?"

"You want me to propose to you?"

"Well, you are the one who brought it up." When she didn't say anything, he grinned. "I'm waiting."

"What, you mean now?"

"There's no time like the present."

"Okay." She cleared her throat. "So will you marry me?

"Now that's pathetic, especially for a lawyer who's supposed to have a way with words."

"Well, what do you want me to say?"

"Something more romantic."

"All right. I love you. Will you marry me?"

He gave a long-suffering sigh, though he was clearly enjoying himself. "I guess if I want something done well, I have to do it myself."

"I *guess*," she answered with a grin, captivated by this new, playful part of his personality.

"Well, if I were going to propose…" He reached over and grabbed Vivian's hands, pulling her against him. "From the first moment I saw you, I knew you were trouble. Too rich, too smart, too beautiful—and you were headed right for me. But never could I have imagined where we would end up. Vivian, I love you. I love everything about you." He smiled ruefully. "Well, everything except your damn money."

"Rafael…"

"The way you smile gets to me. It melts me. And the way you argue for what you believe in. The way you're not afraid to stand up. The way you take the world's problems on your shoulders and still manage to laugh. And love."

He brought her hand to his mouth, placed a lingering kiss in the center of her palm and watched as her eyes went dark and hazy. "I love the way you look at me…and Diego. I love how you always see the big picture and the little details. I love that you're as tough as I am, yet infinitely softer.

"I just love you and I want to spend the rest of my life with you."

Tears were shimmering on her lashes, her breath catching in her throat when he asked, "Will you marry me, Vivian?"

"Yes!" She threw her arms around him and squeezed so tightly that for a second he couldn't tell where she left off and he began. "Yes, yes, yes!"

When she finally let him go, she said, "You know, you're the best Christmas present I ever got."

"Just wait till next year. I'll be a rich man."

"You already are—you have me, don't you?"

"That I do. Thank God."

EPILOGUE

The Following Christmas

"ARE YOU GOING TO OPEN that present or are you just going to stare at it?"

"Yeah, Vivian, hurry up." Michaela smiled at her. "I'm next and I'm dying to check out that big green one with my name on it."

Vivian looked up from the bright red box she held. Rafael's mother had handed it to her with a soft "Feliz Navidad," and she hadn't been able to move since. The package was small and messily wrapped, but it meant more than any present she'd ever received—save the wedding ring Rafael had slipped onto her finger seven months before.

She started to rip the paper delicately, but Gabriel's teasing, "Come on," had her tearing into it like a child. She gasped when she pulled out a scarf as delicate and beautiful as the one she had complimented Michaela on so many months before.

Though it was made of stunning graduated shades of purple silk, it was the intricate beadwork at each end that really captured her attention. It was Michaela's work, she could tell, and the idea that her sister-in-law had gone to the trouble of making her a scarf like this made her feel incredibly special.

But then, everything about being with Rafael made her feel special, important, invincible. It was strange that she'd spent her whole life running from love because she'd been afraid it would make her vulnerable, when the truth was, loving Rafael and accepting his love had made her stronger than she'd ever been.

"It's absolutely stunning, Michaela. Thank you so much."

"You're welcome. Put it on so I can see if I was right about the center color matching your eyes."

Vivian laughed as she draped the scarf around her shoulders.

"It does!" Michaela clapped her hands. "And it highlights them so well."

"It looks great, Vivian." Diego smiled shyly at her from his spot next to the tree, then handed her a package. "Open mine next."

She accepted the small box he handed her and opened it carefully. Inside was a beautifully knit baby blanket. "Oh, Diego, it's gorgeous."

"Esme made it for our baby. I thought it might be nice if you and Rafa could use it for yours."

"We'd be honored, *Uncle* Diego," Rafael said, his hand curving around her waist to rest protectively on the growing mound of her stomach.

Vivian held the blanket long after all the presents had

been opened. And as she watched her newfound family celebrating life and love and Christmas, she thought back on what Rafael had said one year before. Family *was* everything, and she was so grateful to have finally found hers.

Bestselling author Lynne Graham is back with a fabulous new trilogy!

PREGNANT BRIDES

Three ordinary girls—naive, but also honest and plucky...

Three fabulously wealthy, impossibly handsome and very ruthless men...

When opposites attract and passion leads to pregnancy... it can only mean marriage!

Available next month from Harlequin Presents®: the first installment

DESERT PRINCE, BRIDE OF INNOCENCE

* * *

'THIS EVENING I'm flying to New York for two weeks,' Jasim imparted with a casualness that made her heart sink like a stone. 'That's why I had you brought here. I own this apartment and you'll be comfortable here while I'm abroad.'

'I can afford my own accommodation although I may not need it for long. I'll have another job by the time you get back—'

Jasim released a slightly harsh laugh. 'There's no need for you to look for another position. How would I ever see you? Don't you understand what I'm offering you?'

Elinor stood very still. 'No, I must be incredibly thick because I haven't quite worked out yet what you're offering me....'

His charismatic smile slashed his lean dark visage. 'Naturally, I want to take care of you....'

'No, thanks.' Elinor forced a smile and mentally willed him not to demean her with some sordid proposition. 'The only man who will ever take *care* of me with my agreement will be my husband. I'm willing to wait for you to come back but I'm not willing to be kept by you. I'm a very independent woman and what I give, I give freely.'

Jasim frowned. 'You make it all sound so serious.'

'What happened between us last night left pure chaos in its wake. Right now, I don't know whether I'm on my head or my heels. I'll stay for a while because I have nowhere else to go in the short term. So maybe it's good that you'll be away for a while.'

Jasim pulled out his wallet to extract a card. 'My private number,' he told her, presenting her with it as though it was a precious gift, which indeed it was. Many women would have done just about anything to gain access to that direct hotline to him, but his staff guarded his privacy with scrupulous care.

Before he could close the wallet, his blood ran cold in his veins. How could he have made such a serious oversight? What if he had got her pregnant? He knew that an unplanned pregnancy would engulf his life like an avalanche, crush his freedom and suffocate him. He barely stilled a shudder at the threat of such an outcome and thought how ironic it was that what his older brother had longed and prayed for to secure the line to the throne should strike Jasim as an absolute disaster....

* * *

What will proud Prince Jasim do if Elinor is expecting his royal baby? Perhaps an arranged marriage is the only solution! But will Elinor agree? Find out in DESERT PRINCE, BRIDE OF INNOCENCE by Lynne Graham [#2884], available from Harlequin Presents® in January 2010.

HPEX0110B

HARLEQUIN *Presents*

Bestselling Harlequin Presents author

Lynne Graham

brings you an exciting new miniseries:

PREGNANT BRIDES

Inexperienced and expecting, they're forced to marry

Collect them all:

DESERT PRINCE, BRIDE OF INNOCENCE

January 2010

RUTHLESS MAGNATE, CONVENIENT WIFE

February 2010

GREEK TYCOON, INEXPERIENCED MISTRESS

March 2010

REQUEST YOUR FREE BOOKS!

2 FREE NOVELS PLUS 2 FREE GIFTS!

✦ HARLEQUIN®

Super Romance®

Exciting, emotional, unexpected!

YES! Please send me 2 FREE Harlequin® Superromance® novels and my 2 FREE gifts (gifts are worth about $10). After receiving them, if I don't wish to receive any more books, I can return the shipping statement marked "cancel." If I don't cancel, I will receive 6 brand-new novels every month and be billed just $4.69 per book in the U.S. or $5.24 per book in Canada. That's a savings of close to 15% off the cover price! It's quite a bargain! Shipping and handling is just 50¢ per book*. I understand that accepting the 2 free books and gifts places me under no obligation to buy anything. I can always return a shipment and cancel at any time. Even if I never buy another book from Harlequin, the two free books and gifts are mine to keep forever.

135 HDN EYLG   336 HDN EYLS

Name	(PLEASE PRINT)	
Address		Apt. #
City	State/Prov.	Zip/Postal Code

Signature (if under 18, a parent or guardian must sign)

Mail to the **Harlequin Reader Service:**
IN U.S.A.: P.O. Box 1867, Buffalo, NY 14240-1867
IN CANADA: P.O. Box 609, Fort Erie, Ontario L2A 5X3

Not valid to current subscribers of Harlequin Superromance books.

**Are you a current subscriber of Harlequin Superromance books
and want to receive the larger-print edition?
Call 1-800-873-8635 today!**

* Terms and prices subject to change without notice. Prices do not include applicable taxes. Sales tax applicable in N.Y. Canadian residents will be charged applicable provincial taxes and GST. Offer not valid in Quebec. This offer is limited to one order per household. All orders subject to approval. Credit or debit balances in a customer's account(s) may be offset by any other outstanding balance owed by or to the customer. Please allow 4 to 6 weeks for delivery. Offer available while quantities last.

Your Privacy: Harlequin is committed to protecting your privacy. Our Privacy Policy is available online at www.eHarlequin.com or upon request from the Reader Service. From time to time we make our lists of customers available to reputable third parties who may have a product or service of interest to you. If you would prefer we not share your name and address, please check here. ☐

HSR09R

HARLEQUIN® *Blaze*™

New Year, New Man!

*For the perfect New Year's punch,
blend the following:*

- *One woman determined to find her inner vixen*
- *A notorious—and notoriously hot!—playboy*
- *A provocative New Year's Eve bash*
- *An impulsive kiss that leads to a night of
  explosive passion!*

When the clock hits midnight Claire Daniels
kisses the guy standing closest to her, but
the kiss doesn't end after the bells stop ringing....

Look for

Moonstruck

by *USA TODAY* bestselling author

JULIE KENNER

Available January

---

red-hot reads

www.eHarlequin.com

COMING NEXT MONTH

Available January 12, 2010

#1608 AN UNLIKELY SETUP • Margaret Watson
Going Back
Maddie swore she'd never return to Otter's Tail…except she *has* to, to sell the pub bequeathed her, and pay off her debt. Over his dead body, Quinn Murphy tells her. Sigh. If only the sexy ex-cop *would* roll over and play dead.

#1609 HER SURPRISE HERO • Abby Gaines
Those Merritt Girls
They say the cure for a nervous breakdown is a dose of small-town justice. But peaceful quiet is not what temp judge Cynthia Merritt gets when the townspeople of Stonewall Hollow—led by single-dad rancher Ethan Granger—overrule her!

#1610 SKYLAR'S OUTLAW • Linda Warren
The Belles of Texas
Skylar Belle doesn't want Cooper Yates around her daughter. She knows about her ranch foreman's prison record—and treats him like the outlaw he is. Yet when Skylar's child is in danger, she discovers Cooper is the only man she can trust.

#1611 PERFECT PARTNERS? • C.J. Carmichael
The Fox & Fisher Detective Agency
Disillusioned with police work, Lindsay Fox left the NYPD to start her own detective agency. Now business is so good, she needs to hire another investigator. Unfortunately, the only qualified applicant is the one man she can't work with—her ex-partner, Nathan Fisher.

#1612 THE FATHER FOR HER SON • Cindi Myers
Suddenly a Parent
Last time Marlee Britton saw Troy Denton, they were planning their wedding. Then he vanished, leaving her abandoned and pregnant. Now he's returned…and he wants to see his son. Letting Troy back in her life might be the hardest thing she's done.

#1613 FALLING FOR THE TEACHER • Tracy Kelleher
When was Ben Brown last in a classroom? Now his son has enrolled them in a course, so he's giving it his all, encouraged by their instructor, Katarina Zemanova. Love and trust don't come easily, but the lessons yield top marks, especially when they include falling for her!